P9-BIX-555

"I wish I didn't know you were a cop."

Why was it such a big deal to her? It had never made sense to him and it didn't make sense now. Unless she had a record of some kind, unless she was on the run....

He took a step toward her and took her shoulders in his hands, resisting the habit of pulling her into a full embrace. She'd always fit against him perfectly. She was exactly the right height, exactly the right shape, her body a perfect match for his. Even with the baby growing inside her. His baby.

"Why do I want to trust you so much?" she said softly.

"Because somewhere in your heart you know you can."

ALICE SHARPE

A BABY BETWEEN THEM

TORONTO • NEW YORK • LONDON
AMSTERDAM • PARIS • SYDNEY • HAMBURG
STOCKHOLM • ATHENS • TOKYO • MILAN • MADRID
PRAGUE • WARSAW • BUDAPEST • AUCKLAND

If you purchased this book without a cover you should be aware that this book is stolen property. It was reported as "unsold and destroyed" to the publisher, and neither the author nor the publisher has received any payment for this "stripped book."

This book is dedicated to my very dear friend and fellow writer Elisabeth Naughton, with much love.

Recycling programs
for this product may
not exist in your area.

ISBN-13: 978-0-373-74511-1

A BABY BETWEEN THEM

Copyright © 2010 by Alice Sharpe

All rights reserved. Except for use in any review, the reproduction or utilization of this work in whole or in part in any form by any electronic, mechanical or other means, now known or hereafter invented, including xerography, photocopying and recording, or in any information storage or retrieval system, is forbidden without the written permission of the publisher, Harlequin Enterprises Limited, 225 Duncan Mill Road, Don Mills, Ontario, Canada M3B 3K9.

This is a work of fiction. Names, characters, places and incidents are either the product of the author's imagination or are used fictitiously, and any resemblance to actual persons, living or dead, business establishments, events or locales is entirely coincidental.

This edition published by arrangement with Harlequin Books S.A.

® and TM are trademarks of the publisher. Trademarks indicated with ® are registered in the United States Patent and Trademark Office, the Canadian Trade Marks Office and in other countries.

www.eHarlequin.com

Printed in U.S.A.

ABOUT THE AUTHOR

Alice Sharpe met her husband-to-be on a cold, foggy beach in Northern California. One year later they were married. Their union has survived the rearing of two children, a handful of earthquakes registering over 6.5, numerous cats and a few special dogs, the latest of which is a yellow Lab named Annie Rose. Alice and her husband now live in a small rural town in Oregon, where she devotes the majority of her time to pursuing her second love, writing.

Alice loves to hear from readers. You can write her at P.O. Box 755, Brownsville, OR 97327. SASE for reply is appreciated.

Books by Alice Sharpe

HARLEQUIN INTRIGUE
746—FOR THE SAKE OF THEIR BABY
823—UNDERCOVER BABIES
923—MY SISTER, MYSELF*
929—DUPLICATE DAUGHTER*
1022—ROYAL HEIR
1051—AVENGING ANGEL
1076—THE LAWMAN'S SECRET SON**
1082—BODYGUARD FATHER**
1124—MULTIPLES MYSTERY
1165—AGENT DADDY
1190—A BABY BETWEEN THEM

*Dead Ringer
**Skye Brother Babies

Don't miss any of our special offers. Write to us at the following address for information on our newest releases.

Harlequin Reader Service
U.S.: 3010 Walden Ave., P.O. Box 1325, Buffalo, NY 14269
Canadian: P.O. Box 609, Fort Erie, Ont. L2A 5X3

CAST OF CHARACTERS

Simon Task—This lawman has known and loved Ella Baxter for a long time, but he's recently had to admit love isn't always enough. Less than a week after leaving her, she disappears. Now he's either on a fool's errand or the rescue mission of his—and Ella's—life.

Eleanor (Ella) Baxter—She's always been secretive about her past. An auto accident leaves that past a secret from her. The trick becomes surviving events set in motion by an unseen hand. All she's sure of is her determination to reunite with her father and her growing feelings for the "stranger" who comes to her rescue.

Carl Baxter—Ella's husband or maybe her ex-husband. He seems to be caring for her after the accident, but there's no denying his very touch leaves Ella cold. What is he after and how far will he go to get it?

"Chopper"—This big, menacing man wields his knife with deadly accuracy. There is nothing he won't do to get what he wants.

Kyle Starling—Ella's father is a wanted murderer and thief who disappeared from her life many years before. Now he's instigated a deadly chain for Ella to follow—if she can stay alive long enough.

Jack—This larger-than-life man appears out of nowhere. He's a good man to have on your side in a fight. Just what—or who—is he fighting for?

Chapter One

A blob of color off to the left caught Simon Task's attention as he sped out of a town whose name he'd already forgotten.

He immediately pulled off the highway, the truck spraying gravel as he braked to a stop. Swiveling in his seat, he looked back. There it was, a pink-and-orange plastic ladybug, the kind that attached to the top of an automobile antenna. What was it doing buried in a wrecking yard?

His imagination got the worst of him as he waited for a break in the traffic before making a U-turn into the parking lot. He pulled up next to the shell of a rusty van with a shattered windshield.

It had to be a coincidence. There had to be more than one of those silly ladybugs in the world.

His mission, or quest or whatever you wanted to call it, had begun twelve hours earlier when he'd driven by Ella's house at three o'clock in the morning. Since their big fight and their subsequent breakup a few days before, he'd avoided her street, but last night had been a busy one. By the time his shift had ended, he'd been tired enough to take the old shortcut. It wasn't as though she'd be awake to see him drive past.

Much to his surprise, her house had been visible the moment he'd turned the corner, blazing with lights both inside and out. He'd pulled up to the curb in front and sat there until curiosity and uneasiness forced him out of the squad car and up the path to her door.

Wouldn't it be the ultimate irony if the instincts and skills honed on the police force, a job she'd begged him over and over again to quit, now provided the very abilities she depended on to rescue her?

Or was he reading this all wrong?

Wrenching his thoughts back to the present, he caught sight of the small snow globe on the passenger seat and picked it up, twisting his wrist, sending glittery "snow" falling over an otter "floating" on a sea of blue acrylic. On the night he'd found the lights on, he'd gone looking to see if her car was in the garage. No car. Instead, there was the snow globe, all alone where the car should have been, so out of place it caught his eye.

He was here because of this damn snow globe.

But was he in the right place?

He set it back down and got out of the truck, striding toward the fence with determination etched on the lean planes of his face. With his thirty-seventh birthday well behind him, he was a man accustomed to knowing what was going on or moving heaven and earth to find out. First things first.

Rounding a stack of tires, he could finally see through the chain-link fence and what he saw almost froze him in place. The antenna supporting the ladybug mascot was attached to a silver late-model sedan, or what was left of one, the same kind of car Ella drove. The hood was buckled inward and up, all but obscuring the windshield. The passenger compartment was partly crushed, shattered headlights and sprung doors attesting to the power of the impact that had put it here in the first place.

Had the driver walked away from this accident? More to the point—had Ella walked away or was she lying in a morgue somewhere? He swallowed hard. *Make sure it's her car.* Bending at the knees, he perched on his heels as he tried to decipher the bent license plate three feet away. Every letter and number he could make out matched up to Ella's.

"You interested in that car?" a deep voice asked. Simon rose to a standing position as a man popped up from behind a dented SUV, a crowbar in one big hand, two hubcaps tucked under his opposite arm. With a shrill clang, he dropped everything on the rusty hood of yet another wreck and lumbered over to the fence, giving Simon the once-over.

He was fifty or so, pasty and short of breath, a layer of sweat glistening on his brow despite the cool May day. Simon started to reach for his badge but thought better of it. Finding Ella was personal, not official. He said, "It's in pretty bad shape," bracing himself to hear the worst.

"Ain't that the truth?" the man said, producing a can of chewing tobacco. He pinched off a few leaves, tucked the wad in his cheek and added, "Can you believe the driver walked away without a scratch?"

Simon let out a breath he hadn't realized he'd been holding. "Then she's okay?"

"*He's* okay, yeah."

Simon narrowed his eyes. "Wait a second. *He?*"

"The driver. Uninjured except for a scratch or two. Amazing thing. Course, his wife got bonked on the head pretty good. They had an ambulance take her to the hospital." With a wave of a thick arm, he added, "It happened just a mile or two down the road where the highway curves as it drops to the coast. Car went off an embankment and wrapped around a tree."

Okay, just a second. Since when did Ella allow

someone to drive her car, and what was this talk of a husband? "Did you catch any names?"

"Sure. Carl and Eleanor Baxter."

It was on the tip of his tongue to protest that the Eleanor Baxter who owned this car wasn't married. This had to be a mistake. But he paused as he considered her nature. It wasn't inconceivable that she could keep an estranged husband a secret.

He'd actually liked that mysterious quality about her, at least at first. To Simon, coming from a large family with two sisters who never seemed to edit a word they said, Ella had seemed peaceful, composed. It was the churning oceans he'd since detected underneath her calm exterior that grew to worry him.

The wrecker's eyes narrowed. "The Baxters were tourists. How about you? You from around here?"

"No, I'm from Blue Mountain, high desert country. I'm a friend of theirs from back home. Can you tell me how to get to the hospital where Ella, Mrs. Baxter, was taken?"

"If you came from the east, you must have driven right by it. Won't do you no good to look for her there, though. She was released this morning. My wife, Terry, works over there in Housekeeping. She says everyone was surprised Mrs. Baxter left so soon."

Simon's mind was racing. "Was this woman tall with long wavy blond hair?"

"Tall, maybe. Truth is she was in the ambulance by the time I got to the scene. I got a glimpse of her, but her head was wrapped in bandages."

Simon hadn't slept in well over twenty-four hours and he'd been driving for eight. No wonder he couldn't make sense out of anything, no wonder his eyes burned in their sockets. Running a hand through his hair, he said, "Bear with me while I try to understand this. When exactly did the accident happen?"

"Three days ago," the older man said. "In the middle of the night. Every cop in the county showed up along with the fire trucks in case there was an explosion. It was a real circus."

"And the female passenger was released this morning?"

"That's right."

"Do you know if she's still in town? I mean she and her husband?"

The wrecker looked over his shoulder as though he'd suffered a sudden stab of conscience. His wife was no doubt cautioned not to gossip about the patients, but she obviously had and now the wrecker seemed to realize he was repeating her disclosures to a stranger. He spit tobacco with practiced ease, the brown glob landing a few feet away, and scratched his belly through a smudged shirt.

Simon casually took out the leather folder that held his badge. It didn't give him the right to go to the hospital and demand private information without a court order, but he flashed it just the same and the wrecker's face lit up.

"Oh, you're a cop. I get it now. What were they, bank robbers, drug dealers?"

"No, no," Simon said quickly. "I'm just a friend like I told you. I was supposed to meet up with them. I'm showing you the badge so you understand I know how to keep my mouth shut."

The wrecker appeared mildly disappointed. "Well, the answer is they ain't here anymore. Rented a car from Lester down at the Pacific 88 Station, and took off. The husband wanted to continue on their vacation over to Rocky Point."

Rocky Point—Simon had suspected as much. Actually, it had been a toss of the dice, either Otter Cove or Rocky Point, but he'd had a feeling it was the latter. He was itching now to get back in his truck and make it to the coast before dark. One way or another he'd find her. He still didn't know what was going on, just that he needed to see her with his own eyes. If she'd been playing him for a fool the last year or so, well, that was the past, they weren't together anymore anyway.

But he had to know why she'd left the house all lit up and the snow globe in such an odd spot.

The wrecker, meanwhile, had continued rambling and Simon tuned back in to hear him say, "Doctors said as long as he didn't pressure his wife, it probably wouldn't hurt her, and might do her some good. They said it could go away overnight or take a few days or even weeks, just not to push her."

Once again, Simon found himself playing catch-up. "What could go away?" he asked.

"Like I said, her amnesia."

Amnesia? Ella had amnesia? Unsure how to respond to this, Simon worked at looking nonplussed as he racked his brain for a comment that made sense. The wrecker lowered his voice, leaned closer to the fence and added, "The wife heard he's not even supposed to tell her their baby lived through the crash unless she remembers and asks about it."

The shock these words engendered on Simon's face must have shown. The wrecker quickly added, "Her memory better come back pretty damn quick, you ask me."

Okay, this had to be another woman. It wasn't Ella, it couldn't be. Maybe she could have hidden a marriage, but a baby? The sudden image of her perfect nude body, of the taut skin covering her abdomen, flashed in his brain. He'd bet almost anything she'd never given birth.

Now all he had to do was figure out what had happened to Ella to separate her from her car so far from home.

The wrecker added, "My wife said the gal hasn't started showing yet, but nature will take care of that soon enough."

"She's pregnant," Simon blurted out, unable to hide the tremor in his voice.

The wrecker looked pleased with himself. "Yep."

That meant the woman in the car *could* be Ella.

And that meant the baby they were talking about could be *his*.

"IT'S GETTING COLD, Eleanor. Come inside," Carl Baxter called, his voice drifting out to the outdoor balcony through the partially open sliding glass door.

Glancing into the room, Eleanor saw that he'd stretched out atop the king-size bed and was watching the news on television.

"In a minute," she said, wrapping the thin blue sweater closer about her body.

Their room was on the tenth floor and over-looked the Pacific Ocean, the distant horizon flushed with color as the sun plunged toward the sea. The thin wind might be cold, but it was still preferable to being inside the small room with her husband.

Her husband! She absently twisted the gold band on her left hand as she tried yet again to conjure up a memory of Carl that preceded waking up in the hospital. Nothing. But the truth was, it felt funny to think of Carl as her husband. He was good-looking enough, with longish blond hair and an aristocratic face, but there was absolutely nothing about him that spoke to her on any level. He was older than she was, forty-one to her twenty-eight, or so their drivers' licenses revealed. His manner toward her was one of indulgent fondness, she guessed, though it seemed as though he might be a little on the controlling side.

For instance, on the drive from the hospital she'd begged him to drive her home—wherever that might be; no place sounded familiar to her. He'd told her they were going to continue their long-planned road trip, that the doctors had suggested traveling until she regained her memory. They would go back to Blue Mountain when she remembered who she was. It didn't matter that she wanted to go now; the doctors knew best.

Who was she to argue with the doctors? Except this plan seemed backward to her. Wouldn't her own space and belongings trigger a memory or two? And what about her parents or brothers or sisters?

All dead, Carl had told her, and then he'd folded her in his arms as though comforting her, but how was she supposed to mourn people she couldn't even remember?

Her sweater wasn't warm enough for the wind and she fought her reluctance to go inside. She needed better clothes if they were going to stay on the coast. A Windbreaker, for instance. She apparently wasn't much of a packer or maybe her suitcase had been lost in the accident.

She could remember absolutely nothing about the crash. It was as though her head was the inside of a pumpkin: mushy, stringy. The irony of being able to recall the look and smell and taste of a squash but not have a sense of self seemed absurd, and she thought more kindly of Carl. It couldn't be very pleasant to be saddled with a wife in such a befuddled state. She should be grateful to him for standing by her.

But why wouldn't he help her out a little? Why wouldn't he show her pictures or tell her stories about her past or explain what she did for a living, what she liked, what she didn't like?

The doctors. That's why. He was following their orders.

The door opened behind her. Carl stood half in, half out, the wind whipping his hair. Her own short brown locks barely stirred.

"Time to come inside," he said, standing aside to allow her to pass him.

He didn't try to touch her, and for this she was grateful. As she heard the door slide closed behind her, she paused in front of the TV. An announcer was offering details of a homicide, the cameras scanning a weeded lot as a gurney topped with a body bag was wheeled toward a waiting ambulance.

The picture disappeared as Carl clicked the remote. "I was watching that," she said as she turned to face him.

"It happened a long way from here, Eleanor."

"But—"

"I don't want you to watch upsetting, unpleasant things."

She took a deep breath. Was the man always this calculating or had her new vulnerable state aroused his protective instincts? "How long are we staying here?"

"Through Thursday," he said, moving toward her. He put a hand around her arm and, leaning forward, gently kissed her forehead. "You can rest tomorrow. Then the next morning we'll continue on our trip."

"Where exactly are we going?"

"Wherever we want," he said with a smile.

"I want to go home," she said.

"We've been through this a dozen times today," he said.

"Then let's get the map and choose somewhere else to go. I don't like the beach."

"We're staying through tomorrow," he snapped, his eyes flashing even as he resurrected a smile. "Why don't you let me do the planning? You just rest and get better. Are you hungry?"

"Not really. I think I'd like to take a bath."

"You got chilled staying outside so long, didn't you? Well, don't get the bandage on your forehead wet, okay? I'll order dinner from room service."

She resisted nodding, knowing from experience the motion would make her nauseated, then escaped into the bathroom, where she quickly flicked the lock.

Chapter Two

Simon knew he was looking for a blue car with chrome hubcaps, two years old. He knew the license plate number and the fact that it had a green rental sticker in the left corner of the rear window.

Thankfully, Rocky Point wasn't a big town, but it relied heavily on tourists, and as Simon drove into the city, he saw more motels and hotels than he could count. Before the light disappeared altogether, he wanted to cruise parking lots looking for the blue two-door coupe. If the car was parked underground or in a controlled parking lot, he'd be out of luck.

Not for the first time, he wondered if he shouldn't ask for police help. Or maybe he could march up to every front desk in town and demand to know if there was a Carl and Eleanor Baxter registered. But all of that came with official ramifications, and for now he didn't want anyone else involved. He knew if he started waving his badge around in a town this small, it wouldn't be long before the local cops came looking for him—no, thanks.

The beginning letters on the plate he sought were *YSL*. He pulled into a motel on the beach and drove each row as though looking for a parking place, slowing down at every blue car. Who knew there wcrc so damn many of them?

An hour passed, then two. He drove through a fast food restaurant and ordered a hamburger and black coffee, then went back to his task, gradually working his way north through town.

The task seemed impossible and more than once he was on the brink of taking a room, getting some sleep and heading home in the morning. But he kept at it, more out of perverse determination than because he thought his plan held merit.

A dozen lots later, his eyes burning like red-hot embers, his headlights picked up the letters *YSL* attached to a blue coupe. He pulled into a spot a few cars away and walked back. The rest of the plate checked out, too; the green sticker was right where it belonged. He used his pocket flashlight to briefly scan the interior. There was nothing in the car he could see except a road map.

He grabbed his overnight bag from his truck and walked into the hotel. It was eleven o'clock by now and the place was all but deserted. He toyed around with asking the clerk who gave him a room if they had a couple named Baxter registered, but held off—he didn't want Baxter alerted to his presence until he got a feeling for what was going on.

A few minutes later, he let himself into his room with the intent of taking a shower and then casing the hotel. He sat on the bed and pulled off his shoes.

If Ella was the woman in the car, then she was here, in the same building as he. Was her memory completely gone? Before that had happened to her, had she really left clues in the hope he would figure out she needed him, or had he jumped to a bunch of conclusions?

No. She might have lent her car to someone else, but she certainly hadn't willingly lent her identity. So who was the man acting as her husband and why had he brought an amnesic woman on a vacation instead of taking her home?

He took the snow globe out of his overnight bag and turned it in his hands, remembering the day a few months before when he and Ella had bought it at a gift store less than a mile from here.

Back when they'd been a couple.

Rubbing his eyes, he fell back on the bed and stared up at the ceiling. *She was here.* He could almost feel her presence. When he'd walked out on their argument just days before, he'd intended it to be permanent, but here he was and so was she.

Which added complicated dimensions to the

question burning in the back of his brain: What in the hell was going on?

He woke up hours later, still lying on his back, gray morning light filtering through the sheer curtains. "Damn," he muttered as he tore off his clothes on the way to the bathroom. Five minutes later, he'd taken the fastest shower since his stint in the navy and caught an elevator to the lobby. He immediately crossed to the windows to see if the blue car was still in the parking lot. If he'd slept through their departure, what would he do next?

What could he do?

ELEANOR STARED AT THE PLATE of food Carl had ordered against her wishes and felt a wave of sickness rise up her throat. Thank goodness they were in their room and not the dining room.

"What's wrong?" Carl said.

She didn't have time to answer. Throwing her hand over her mouth, she ran to the bathroom and was sick. Sometime later, after she'd washed and brushed her teeth, she wandered back.

"I thought you could eat," he said.

"My stomach—"

"The doctor warned you'd be sick off and on again due to your head injury," he said.

"Well, the doctors were right." The smell of the congealing eggs was making her stomach tumble again. She grabbed her handbag off the chair. She'd searched her purse; she knew she had credit cards in the wallet. "Give me the car keys. I need different clothes and I need to get out of this room," she said, her hand on the knob.

He was grabbing his jacket. "I'll go with you."

It was on the tip of her tongue to add, *I need to get away from you most of all!* Instead she said, "I remember how to drive. The town didn't look that big yesterday—I can make my way."

She stopped talking because he'd put on his jacket and held the keys in his fist. "No, Eleanor, you will not drive yourself around with a head injury. I'll take you wherever you want to go. Besides, mine is the only name on the rental. You're not insured."

"Then I'll walk."

"Don't be absurd."

And because her head throbbed and her stomach roiled, she opened the door and left the room, Carl close on her heels.

It was a drizzly day outside. As Carl went to the front desk, she perused the lobby. Several people were standing or sitting in chairs in front of a big, hooded fireplace. She longed to be one of them, longed to go stand by the fire without Carl hovering nearby.

Her gaze met the gray eyes of a man in his

thirties. He was tall and solid-looking, wearing boots, jeans and a black sweater. His hair was dark and thick, combed away from his face. His features were attractive, his mouth perfectly formed, but it was the intensity of his gaze that held her, that sent her left hand up to her cheek. His gaze grew even more piercing and a trill of excitement sputtered along her skin.

She looked away at once, but for some reason looked back. He had turned to stare at the fire.

"Ready?" Carl asked.

She startled.

"The clerk at the desk told me there's a nice clothing store less than a mile from here. Come on."

SIMON WAITED UNTIL HE SAW the taillights go on in their car before he left the building and ran to his truck. Within a few moments he'd caught up with them on the main drag.

A brisk, overcast Tuesday morning in April wasn't exactly high tourist time, he discovered, and wished there were a few more cars around. He'd already announced himself by allowing Ella to notice him staring at her. He couldn't afford another sighting.

But he hadn't been able to take his eyes off her. Her hair was short and dark, a fringe of bangs somewhat obscuring bruises and a bandage, framing her deep blue eyes. She'd looked wistful, vulnerable in a way he'd seen her look so few times. He'd wanted to walk up to her, talk with her, see if she knew who he was, ask her to explain what was happening.

Of course, he hadn't, and when she'd raised her hand to her face in an almost shy gesture, he finally noticed the sparkle of gold on her finger.

She wore a wedding ring. And the man who had come up to her wore one, too. A tall man with long fair hair, chiseled features and a hustler's tilt to his head.

Damn.

Simon hung back a block until he saw the turn signal on the rental. By the time he turned the same corner, the man was helping Ella out of the car. Simon pulled up to the curb half a block away and watched as they entered a building.

The man. Ella's husband. Carl Baxter. Call him what he was. But why had Ella dyed her hair? She had to have done it before the accident; surely she wouldn't use dye with scratches and wounds on her head, but again, why? Her hair was a source of pride for her, at least it had been, so why whack it off unless to disguise herself?

After getting rid of you, maybe she just wanted a change, an inner voice suggested.

Simon pulled his sweater over his head and put

on the denim jacket he kept in the backseat, then snatched a green baseball cap out of a side pocket. As disguises went, it wasn't great, but it was as good as he could do without risking losing them, and he wasn't going to chance that. He darted across the street.

The inside of the store wasn't exactly booming with customers, but it was jammed with racks of clothes that seemed to go from floor to ceiling. The clutter made lurking a little safer. He'd just make sure they were in here to actually look at clothes, and then he'd leave and stake out the exterior.

Cap pulled low on his forehead, he caught sight of Ella fingering a rack of blue-green sweaters. It was his favorite color on her.

She took one of the sweaters off the rack and held it up against her supple body, the soft material at once clinging to her breasts and evoking a million erotic memories. It was a long garment and as she turned to look at herself in the mirror, he felt his breath catch in his throat. The night they first met came stampeding into his head and heart like a locomotive off its tracks.

Carl Baxter chose that moment to take the blue sweater from her hands and thrust a yellow one at her.

Simon immediately turned around and left the store, retracing his steps to the truck, where he took out his cell phone. He made two calls. One to work to request a few days' vacation and the other to an old friend. Then he hunkered down to wait.

"YOU LOOK BEAUTIFUL," Carl said, placing his hands on her shoulders and leaning down to kiss the nape of her neck. He was standing behind her as she faced the mirror, trying to arrange her hair to hide her abrasions and bandages.

She didn't really like the look of the yellow against her skin, and Carl's lips left her cold, which made her ashamed of herself. As he raised his head and their gazes locked in the reflection of the mirror, she said, "Do we have a good marriage, Carl?"

He smiled. "Of course we have a good marriage."

"Then why won't you tell me about it? You know, about one of our days, maybe. A Saturday, for instance. Tell me what we do on a Saturday when I don't have to go to work at the…"

He laughed. "Trying to trick me into telling you what you do for a living?"

"Can't you just throw me a bone? What do you do for a living?"

"Why this preoccupation with jobs?"

"I don't know, I just feel so lost waiting around, I want to do something. I want to know what I used to do, what we did as a couple."

He moved away toward the door. "Let's go."

"Carl—"

"You haven't eaten all day. You must be starving."

"But the reservation—"

"Is for an hour from now, I know, but they serve wine and cheese before dinner in the lobby. A little wine will do you good."

"With my head injury?" she said.

"One glass won't hurt."

There was just no point in arguing with him. The man never said or did one thing he didn't want to say or do, seldom let her out of his sight. *We better have a good marriage,* she thought as she walked past him into the hall, *because if we don't, I'm going to divorce him when I get my memory back.*

Though she would hardly admit it to herself, there was someone she was hoping to see again and that was the man from the morning. He wasn't in the lobby, however. She took a seat near the fire, the gray late-afternoon skies pressing against the tall windows at her back. Carl walked over to the informal buffet as she looked around the spacious room, glancing at the half dozen other guests sipping wine and laughing.

What would it be like to laugh? Did she laugh a lot? Was she morose or happy or contemplative?

One thing Carl was right about was the return

of her appetite. It was back with a vengeance, and as she accepted a small plate covered with cheese and crackers and grapes, she noticed a tall man walk into the lobby from the outside and veer toward the front desk.

"Wine?" Carl said, and she accepted a glass of chilled white wine and set it on the table next to her plate. He stood by her seat, looking down at her as he sipped a dark red Cabernet and she tried a cracker slathered with creamy Brie. Why didn't he sit, why did he hover? She looked surreptitiously toward the desk, but the tall man was gone.

It had been the man from the morning, she was sure of it, the one with the gray eyes.

At that moment, a woman approached Carl. "Are you Mr. Baxter?" she asked.

He looked down his long nose at the woman who was wearing a hotel uniform identifying her as an employee. "Yes."

"Sir, we've been alerted your car has two very flat front tires. Would you come with me?"

Carl looked down at Eleanor and then back at the employee and said, "Just have it fixed. I'm not leaving my wife alone—"

"Oh, for heaven's sake, Carl," Eleanor snapped. "I'm not a child, I think I can sit here for ten minutes while you take care of an emergency."

He looked toward the parking lot, down at

her and back again. The employee said, "It'll only take a few minutes, sir. We need insurance information."

"It's your damn parking lot," Carl fumed.

"Yes, sir, but it's well posted that your car is your responsibility. Not that we won't assist you, of course."

Carl set his glass down beside Eleanor's. "Stay here," he commanded, and marched off behind the woman and out the front door, glancing over his shoulder at Eleanor twice before he was out of sight.

Almost at once, a man sat on the chair beside her. His gray gaze delving right into hers, he said, "Your husband seems upset."

"It's you," she said, and realizing how lame that sounded, added, "I saw you this morning."

"I saw you, too," he said.

"You were staring at me."

"Yes. Well, I thought you might be someone I knew."

She leaned forward a little. "Really? Maybe I am."

"I don't quite get your meaning," he said with a smile, his voice playful.

She shrugged. "I had an accident a few days ago and my memory is a little blurred."

"A little?"

"A lot."

His voice dropped as he said, "Is that why your husband never leaves your side?"

She nodded very slowly and reached for her wineglass. The stranger's hand was suddenly there, as well. Somehow her glass sailed to the floor, spilling its contents. "I'm sorry," he said, producing a napkin or two and blotting her shoe. The rest of the liquid was quickly absorbed into the plush carpet. He set the unbroken glass back on the table and added, "Probably better not to drink when you've recently bashed your head, I suppose."

"I agree. I really didn't want it."

"Then why were you reaching for it?"

She met his eyes and smiled. "Because I didn't know how to respond to your observation about my husband. Have you ever noticed how you tend to do something with your hands when you don't know what to say?"

"I have noticed that," he said, his gaze once again penetrating. She should probably look away. She couldn't. Their conversation was harmless enough, but she found herself enjoying it in a way she hadn't enjoyed anything in days. She liked talking to this man. He made her feel something inside, made her feel less alone. "What's your name?" she asked.

"Simon."

"Just Simon?"

He brushed her gold wedding band with his fingertip. "Just Simon. What's yours?"

"Eleanor."

He withdrew his hand and she swallowed. Her reactions to this guy were giving her one of the few glimpses she'd had of her gut-level personality. She wore one man's ring and that man swore they had a good marriage. And yet she flirted with another man and wished she had no husband.

"Tell me about the woman you thought I resembled," she said.

Simon glanced toward the front door and then back at her. "I was in love with her once," he said.

"That sounds sad. Something happened between you?"

"Yes. Something happened."

"What was she like?"

"Well, let's see. She was very pretty, like you. She liked to garden, especially vegetables. Everything grew for her. And she liked to cook."

"She sounds like a homebody," Eleanor said.

"Kind of, yes."

"What did she do, you know, for a living?"

"She worked at a radio station, had her own show in the afternoons on Saturday. Gardening tips, food advice, stuff like that. She also had a slew of odd jobs because she said she didn't want to get stuck doing one thing forever."

"What kind of odd jobs?"

"Once she painted a mural on the side of an office building and once she walked dogs and house-sat. She also taught a few classes at the junior college and volunteered at an old folks' home. Stuff like that."

Eleanor smiled. "She sounds nice. What happened, you know, between you two?" As he looked away from her face, she chided herself and added, "I'm sorry. That was way too personal. I don't remember anything about myself, so maybe that's why I'm so caught up in hearing about this woman you're describing. Don't tell me any more, it's none of my business."

He opened his mouth, seemed to think better, and closed it. "How long are you staying here, Eleanor?"

"Until tomorrow," she said. "Carl insisted we stay through today."

"Then where are you headed? Home?"

"I wish," she said.

"You sound homesick. Been away long?"

"How do I know?" she said, turning beseeching eyes on him. "I don't know for sure when we left home or even exactly where home is except for the address on my driver's license."

"You don't remember anything about it?"

"No. The address on my husband's license is

different from mine. When I asked him why, he told me we've moved recently. That's all he'll say."

"If you want to go home so badly, why don't you?"

"Because the doctor said we should stay away until my memory returns. Carl won't tell me anything about myself. He says it's supposed to come back naturally."

"Makes it kind of hard for you, doesn't it?" he said.

"I feel lost."

"I bet you do," he said, his gaze once again holding hers.

"How about you?" she said softly.

"I'm not sure about my plans, either." His gaze swiveled to the doors again, and he got to his feet quickly. "I see your husband stomping across the parking lot. He looks pretty angry."

"I'm beginning to think he's angry quite often," she said, instantly awash in guilt. She added, "He's taking very good care of me. It can't be much fun for him."

"You underestimate yourself," he said, and then as Carl pushed his way through the front doors, the man with the gray eyes disappeared toward the elevators.

Simon was right. Carl looked mad enough to kill someone.

Chapter Three

"So you agree she shouldn't be told she's pregnant?"

On the other end of the line, his cousin Virginia, a practicing psychologist in Chicago, paused for a second before saying, "Without knowing the specifics of her case, I don't know what to think. In associational therapy, the patient is exposed to familiar surroundings in hopes it stimulates the brain's neural synapses. Isolation from personal recollections seems counterintuitive, but if you know she's pregnant and sense trouble in her marriage—"

"If there is a marriage," Simon interjected.

"You said your partner on the force is checking into that, right?"

"Not my partner, no. I can't get Mike into a compromising position on the off chance Ella did something illegal before she left Blue Mountain." *Or since then, for that matter....*

"Then who did you call?"

"A private investigator I worked with a few years back."

"You're sure Ella isn't faking amnesia?"

"I'm positive. The only way the woman I know could react to things the way this woman does is if she wasn't aware of herself or her past. She's not faking."

"Okay. So, for now, all you know is she's with a man who was able to convince the police and the hospital he's her husband, which means he either planned her abduction very carefully or he is her husband—"

"In which case there is no mystery, just me jumping to conclusions," Simon finished for her. And yet her husband had told Ella they'd just moved to Blue Mountain, which was a lie. Ella had lived there for at least two or three years.

Virginia cleared her throat. "Didn't your mother tell me you and Ella were no longer a couple? In fact, you broke up with her just a week or so ago, didn't you?"

Simon stared out at the ocean and sighed. "Well, I guess you could say I broke up with her. She'd gotten even more secretive than usual and we had some words and I realized it was over."

"So maybe what you're feeling is guilt mixed with anger," she said softly.

"Huh?"

"Guilt for rejecting her. Then you find she has a husband all along and so really, she's the one who rejected you. That's why she wouldn't talk about her past and why you felt shut out of her life. Hence the anger."

"My mother has a big mouth."

"She talks to my mom, you know how it is."

He glowered at the moon sparkling over the sea and didn't respond. Spending the night staking out the parking lot wasn't his idea of a good time, but he figured it would serve a couple of purposes, and face it, he was anxious to get this settled in his mind and go home.

Home. "Ginny, do you think I should tell Ella who I am and ask her if she wants to come back with me? Give her a choice?"

"No. I can't advise distressing her when she's so lost already. Don't do anything to alarm her or frighten her. Listen, do you want me to call the admitting hospital and see if I can find out anything about her condition?"

"Will they talk to you?"

"I'll give it a try. I might know someone here who knows someone there. Call me back tomorrow night about this time, okay? Her name is Eleanor Baxter, right?"

"Yeah. Middle name Ann. Thanks, Ginny."

"Just be careful."

"Careful? Careful of what?"

"Think about it, coz," she said, and rang off.

He pocketed his cell phone and tried to get comfortable. He was parked across the row and three cars down from the Baxter rental so he could easily keep an eye on it.

And then he did his best not to think about Ella, but that was almost impossible.

She was different and it wasn't just the hair color. She was more open, as though not remembering her past had freed her from the burden of keeping it secret. She reminded him of the woman he'd fallen in love with, practically at first sight.

He got the feeling she wasn't too happy about her husband. For that matter, neither was Simon, who had seen the bastard hand Ella that glass of wine. Ella didn't know she was pregnant, but according to the wrecker's wife, Carl did, so what was he doing giving a pregnant woman alcohol?

That was Simon's baby she was carrying, and it pissed him off.

At least he thought it was his baby.

But she'd been hiding something for the past couple of weeks, something that had her edgy, nervous...

He switched positions. He had a feeling he wasn't going to get Ella alone again. The tire trick had worked once; it wouldn't work again without arousing suspicion. The fact that Carl had insisted they continue this vacation and stay in Rocky Point made Simon curious. What if Carl had abducted Ella from her house in Blue Mountain? What if the accident had been just that—an accident? Had Carl pushed for her release from the hospital so they could make it to Rocky Point for some unknown reason? Or what if they were in something together but Ella couldn't remember they were partners? Would that explain her changed appearance?

It all came down to her houselights blazing, the abandoned snow globe in the garage and his gut feeling.

No answers right now, maybe tomorrow. He'd watch them come out to the car in the morning. See if Ella, once out of the hotel, appeared to be in distress. If she did, he would call in the cops.

"Be careful," Ginny had said.

To hell with that. Carl Baxter was the one who better be careful.

Using his pocket flashlight, he opened the paperback he'd bought in the hotel gift shop and prepared for a long night.

"LET'S STOP HERE for breakfast," Carl said as he pulled into the deep unpaved parking lot belonging to a restaurant perched high above the ocean. A fog bank hovered out at sea, though the day had dawned clear but breezy. The few trees managing to cling to the bluff were shaped by the predominant winds.

"I'll stay here, you go eat," Eleanor said. "My stomach feels terrible. It must be that pill I take at night, the one for my head. I wake up every morning with a stomachache."

"Then skip the pill tonight," he said, reaching over to unbuckle her seat belt.

"Carl, I can't eat."

He looked at his watch, then at her. There was something different about him today, a tightening around his mouth and eyes. "How selfish can you get?" he snarled. "Do you think just because you can't eat, I should starve?"

Startled, she drew away from him. "You could have ordered from room service."

"I'm tired of room service. Come on, get out of the car, keep me company. We'll get you some toast."

She got out of the car, unsure why she allowed him to bully her. Was this what she was always like, or was this apathy because of her injuries? She hoped and prayed it was the latter, because the woman she was right now was a tiresome bore who had come to life only once since awakening and that was when she spoke with a stranger about his lost love.

How pathetic was that?

A bell tinkled as they opened the door. The restaurant was bigger inside than it had looked from the outside. Tables ringed the perimeter, which was fronted with glass and a panoramic view of the sea beyond.

Waitresses scurried with giant platters perched on their shoulders; others poured endless cups of coffee. A hostess led them to a table near the windows. Eleanor took a chair facing the door as the waitress handed them menus. "Coffee?" she asked.

"Just one cup," Carl said. "The lady wants tea."

As the waitress hurried off, Carl scooted his chair clear around the table so that he was facing the door, too. He said, "Now, aren't you glad you came inside?"

She looked at the menu while taking shallow breaths. The place smelled like greasy seafood. Refusing to lie about her supposed joy at being talked into coming inside, she folded the menu. Carl looked up at the door, visibly tensing every time the bell announced a newcomer.

"Are you expecting someone?" she asked.

"Expecting? No. Why do you ask?"

"You keep staring at the door."

"So what?" he said.

His attitude toward her had taken a marked change from the preceding days. No longer overly solicitous, he was directing his general impatience at her. Truth was, she almost preferred it.

The waitress arrived with two coffees. As Eleanor had no plans to drink tea or anything else, she didn't comment on the mistake. Carl didn't seem to notice. "Crab omelet is our special today," the waitress chirped.

"That's fine," Carl said absently, twisting a little as a bell announced a family scurrying in out of the wind.

"Nothing for me," Eleanor said.

"Bring her unbuttered toast," Carl said.

The family was seated a table or two away while a man in a green baseball cap with his nose buried in a blue-and-white handkerchief took a seat at a table behind her. Carl finally noticed her beverage. "They brought you coffee? Why didn't you say something? Where is that stupid waitress?"

"It doesn't matter," she assured him. His nerves were beginning to get to her, too. Trying to soothe him, she looked around and added, "This is a nice restaurant. Maybe we could come back tonight and have dinner here."

"I suspect we'll be long gone before that," he said absently, tensing as the bell rang over the door again.

A different waitress appeared with a tray holding a tall stack of pancakes and a pitcher of syrup. As she started to lower the tray, Carl put up a hand. "I didn't order pancakes," he barked. "You've got the wrong table."

The tray tilted precariously as the waitress attempted to check the ticket buried in her apron pocket. Carl yelled at her, and she jerked. With a clatter, the plate slid right off the platter and landed in Carl's lap. The pitcher of syrup followed.

Carl stood abruptly, his face as red as a boiled Dungeness crab.

The waitress immediately began apologizing and dabbing at Carl with a napkin.

"You clumsy oaf," Carl sputtered, pushing her away.

"Sir, breakfast will be on us, of course."

"It's already on me!" he said, lifting his sticky hands. "Damn, I've got to go to the restroom and try to fix this." His gaze went from his watch to the door to Eleanor. "Stay here. I'll be back in two minutes." He stomped off without waiting for a reply.

SIMON, NURSING A CUP of coffee and hiding behind a menu, watched the incident at Ella's table with interest. He was willing to bet a week's pay the waitress purposely dumped the food on Carl Baxter.

Why?

That question was at least partially answered a moment later when an Albert Einstein look-alike slid into the chair across from Ella. As the waitress shuffled off with the spilt food and dishes, Simon carefully shifted position to sit directly behind Ella in order to eavesdrop.

"Good, you made it," the old guy said, his voice raspy. "Sorry about the mess with your friend, but I wanted to talk to you alone."

Eleanor said, "I'm sorry, but—"

"Do you know anything about Jerry? Last anyone heard from him was the day he came to see you."

"I don't—"

"Never mind, Jerry is clever, he can take care of himself. What's important is you. I'm real sorry about your brother. Oh, I know it's been months since his death, but I still remember him as a cute kid with a real gung ho attitude. Tragic thing to die so young."

Ella had a brother? This was news to Simon, who cursed his decision not to run a check on her background when he had had the chance.

"Okay, I'm stalling and we don't have much time," the old man continued. "Like Jerry told you, your dad set up this roundabout way of getting word to you to protect you and him. Jerry got you this far. My job is to tell you about the next stop. Go north to a suburb of Seattle named

Tampoo. Be at the bus depot tomorrow right at noon. We all know what you look like. Come alone next time, okay?"

"I don't—"

"Listen, honey, there's a lot to explain, but don't ask me, I'm just a link in the chain. You need to ask your old man. You be careful now, it's likely to get dangerous before the end." The old guy looked up just then and after quietly patting the table three times with his fingertips, he got to his feet. "Don't let your father down," he said, and quickly faded into the shadows toward the kitchen.

Ella hadn't seen a man come out of the bathroom and pull on his ear, but Simon had. That was a signal if he'd ever seen one, and it was followed within seconds by the appearance of Carl Baxter, a determined glint in his eyes and water spots on his clothes. Simon dived behind the menu again.

There was no time to trail the old man; he had to stay and hear what Ella said to Carl about this visit. His hope was she would say nothing.

"The strangest thing just happened," Ella said as another waitress arrived with a plate of eggs she set in front of Carl and toast she placed in front of Ella.

Worried Carl would start looking at the door again and notice Simon's interest in him, Simon turned his back completely, staring out at the sea and the encroaching fog. He heard Carl say, "What? What happened?"

"An old man sat down and spoke with me. He said something about my father."

"What did you say to him?" Carl asked, his voice fast and higher pitched than before.

"Nothing. I mean, what could I say?"

"The man must have mistaken you for someone else. Maybe he's a nutcase."

"Maybe," Ella said, "but he implied he had something to do with the food being spilled on you."

The bell on the door chimed and Simon glanced over his shoulder to get Carl's reaction. Carl didn't even look up. Instead he said, "Tell me what the old guy said."

Don't tell him anything, Simon chanted to himself.

"Well, he told me my father needed me. I thought you told me all my family was dead."

"He's a nutcase, just as I thought." A brief pause was followed by "So, did the old guy mention a city and a time?"

"Yes. Tampoo, Washington, tomorrow at noon. At a bus depot. He said someone would meet me. He said I should go alone. What does that mean?"

"How would I know?" Carl said with a clatter of silverware. "You're not eating, and I'm not hungry anymore. Let's get out of here."

Ella's voice was very calm as she said, "What's going on, Carl? How did you know he mentioned going to another city?"

"I didn't, you just told me."

"No, you asked. It's a strange question. I may not remember who I am, but I didn't suddenly get stupid."

"Just put your coat on. I'll explain in the car."

Simon heard chairs slide and watched as Ella stalked out of the restaurant. Carl stood by the cash register, glancing repeatedly outside as though afraid Ella would fly away. When no waitress appeared to take his money, he tossed a few bills on the counter and left. He'd apparently forgotten the waitress promised him a free meal.

Simon slapped a couple of dollars next to his empty coffee mug and followed, pulling on his cap, unsure how to proceed. If he'd been confused before, he was downright flummoxed now, but he also sensed Ella might be in danger from this man as she began to suspect his motives.

Ginny had said don't alarm Ella, don't frighten her. How was he supposed to get her away from Carl if he couldn't even talk to her?

He exited the restaurant with his head down so Ella wouldn't notice him. A quick glance, however, revealed that she'd made it to their car, which was parked close to the bluff. She stood with her back to the restaurant and to Carl's approach, arms linked across her chest, one hip thrust forward, her short, dark hair barely moving despite the strong wind. A lilac-colored coat flapped around her hips.

Her body language screamed *pissed off.* The bounce of Carl's steps and the faint whistling sound drifting back on the wind suggested Carl couldn't care less about his wife's frame of mind.

The weather had deteriorated, the thin fog blowing up the bluff, swirling overhead. Searching for an excuse to approach Carl before he talked Ella into getting into the car, Simon noticed movement in a dark sedan parked nearby. The door opened as Carl passed the front bumper. Carl didn't even turn to look as a big man with a very bushy gray-streaked beard got out of the car.

The huge man was dressed all in black and looked damn formidable as he peered around the parking lot, his gaze sliding right by Simon, whose instincts had warned him to step behind a pillar. Apparently making a decision, the giant fell into step behind Carl.

It didn't take Simon's twelve years in law enforcement to figure out something was going on.

Picking up his pace, the bearded man grabbed Carl from behind, twirling him around, throwing a punch that connected with Carl's nose. As he staggered backward, Carl pulled a gun from a hidden holster. The bearded man instantly kicked the gun from Carl's hand with an agility unexpected in a three-hundred-pound man. The gun flew over the bluff as the assailant produced a terrible, mean-looking knife with a curved blade.

Ella screamed. Simon started running toward her, taking his own gun from the waistband holster. Facing each other, jockeying for position, the two men backed Ella against the car. She pushed them away from her, lurching off to the side as blood from a knife slash blossomed on her palm. It ran down her arm as she continued stumbling backward.

Again and again, the bearded man swung his knife in wide arcs at Carl. Ella seemed oblivious of anything but the fight. The men kept at it, forcing her toward the edge of the bluff as the giant lashed out and Baxter recoiled.

Birds wheeling up the bluff caught Simon's attention. At once he realized the direction Ella's retreat was taking her. He yelled her name. The two men turned to look at him, but Ella kept moving as though oblivious of anything except escape. She stumbled backward against the knee-high rock and wood post wall, her hands flying, her purse launched into the air. She'd been moving so fast her momentum sent her sailing over the edge of the fog-shrouded cliff.

Both men lurched toward the bluff, became aware of each other again, and squared off. Carl peered at the empty spot where Ella had last appeared, obviously caught between his desire to find out what had happened to her and the one to save his own skin.

His skin won. He used the big man's momentary lapse of attention to get a head start back to his car.

Simon was only vaguely aware of the two men taking off in their respective vehicles as he reached the place where Ella had tumbled over the cliff.

Chapter Four

The bluff was riddled with gullies and overgrown with Scotch broom, their brilliant yellow flowers dazzling despite the fog. More important than their color was the fact that they could cushion, maybe even stop, a fall.

"Ella!"

Twenty feet below him, he caught sight of movement, but it was impossible to tell if a person was responsible or if it was just the wind rattling the tortured boughs of a Sitka spruce.

Slapping his revolver back in the holster, Simon climbed over the fence and onto the narrow ledge, calling her name again. To his infinite relief, he heard her voice.

"Help! Someone help!"

As he took a cautious step, the sandy rocks beneath his feet shifted and he slipped. He grabbed one of the wood posts and caught himself but not before a shower of rocks skittered down the gully.

"Hold on!" he yelled.

Leaving her there was one of the hardest things he'd ever done, but he had to get a rope or risk stranding them both. He knew exactly where it was in his truck and dug his keys out as he ran. It was over twenty miles back to town. A call to the fire station would set a rescue in motion. Should he take the time to fiddle with his phone and instigate it?

No.

Grabbing the rope, he ran back across the lot. There was no one else around.

Fingers steady, he quickly rigged a bowline in the rope and hitched it over the wood post six feet north of where he figured Ella had landed or caught hold of a branch or root. The fate of the baby she carried flashed across his mind, but he let it go. There was nothing he could do except save Ella.

"Ella?" he yelled as he tore off the green baseball cap and pulled on the work gloves he'd grabbed along with the rope.

It took her forever to answer and when she did, her voice was faint. "Hurry. I can't hold on much longer."

"Keep talking. I'm rappelling down to your left, so no rocks will hit you, but I can't see in the fog. I don't know exactly where you are."

"I'm kind of in a tree," she called, her voice a little stronger.

The cliff below the post he'd chosen wasn't gullied like the other, but stuck out in weathered bare rock. Leaning backward and paying out the rope through his gloved hands, Simon backed down the face until his feet hit empty air. He swung back against the cliff, the impact briefly knocking the wind out of his lungs.

Below him and to his right, he heard Ella yell, "Are you okay?"

"Keep talking," he sputtered, and immediately pushed himself away. Now he could start veering toward the sound of Ella's voice as she recited the alphabet, catching his feet in the gullies and fending off the brush as it became more dense. At last he spied a glimpse of lilac that almost but not quite blended in with the foliage.

Ella was wearing a jacket that color.

Another foot or two and he could see the gleaming cap of her brown hair and then two wide blue eyes.

She'd been stopped from the three-hundred-foot drop to the surf below by the branches of the spruce, themselves twisted by the wind. She clung to the end of a slender branch, one leg looped over the top, both hands clinging to the rough bark. The tree didn't look all that sturdy, but the thick foliage above her head explained why he hadn't been able to see her from above.

Pushing with his legs, he swung toward her, landing on the bluff right below her dangling foot.

"You have to let go," he said. The sound of the surf seemed twice as loud as it had from the top of the bluff and he raised his voice, reaching up to touch her denim-covered leg. "Trust me."

She looked down at him but hesitated. He wondered if she recognized him. Even if she did, why would she trust him? She didn't remember she knew him, and the basic Ella he'd come to understand was a woman who liked to control her own destiny and didn't trust easily.

"You sure that rope is strong enough for both of us?" she called.

He knew the rope was strong enough. They'd soon find out if the wood post at the top was. He said, "Would you rather hang around here all day?"

The tree creaked as she adjusted her weight. "Okay, point taken. Just be ready."

"I'll manage. Go slow. Keep a good grip on the tree as long as you can. Use me like a ladder. When you get down here where I can grab you around your waist, we'll figure out how to get back up the cliff, okay?"

"Okay," she said, and slowly began unhooking her death grip from the tree. He braced himself, tying off the rope around his waist so he could use both hands to grab her. Within a few moments, her foot hit his shoulder and his fingers wrapped around her calf. She all but slithered down his body until she paralleled him, one arm swung around his neck. The palm of her other hand was still bleeding and her clothes were splotched with blood.

She craned her neck and looked into his eyes. "What are *you* doing here?" Her voice was hushed and amazed.

"Saving you," he said. "Hold on," he added as he pushed them away from the bluff, shifting his weight to the left, landing a few feet back toward the direction he'd descended from. Ella caught on quickly and helped him by synchronizing her body movements to his, though he still wasn't sure how he was going to climb hand over hand up this rope with her in tow.

He heard voices from above.

"Who's up there?" she whispered, her breath warm against his neck. Hell of a time to feel a surge of sexual recognition.

"I have no idea," he muttered. There was suddenly new tension on the rope. Had some Good Samaritan figured out they needed help? "Other than your hand, are you hurt?"

"I don't think so." She glanced between their feet and added, "Just scared."

"Don't look," he cautioned, though he knew from his own brief glance all she could really see was thick fog creeping through the brush and trees. It was the faraway sound of the crashing surf that was alarming.

More voices drifted down the bluff, and the rope slowly started pulling them upward. "Hold on to the rope with your good hand and me with the other," he said. "Try to keep your feet against the cliff and walk with the rope." He didn't add that he hoped whoever was up there knew not to go too fast.

The most harrowing part was the last bump of rock that meant they hung suspended for what seemed an eternity, but after their feet hit the ground again it was simply a matter of taking the last few steps.

At the top, people reached for Ella and for him. Simon saw his rope had been tied to the towing wrench on a big four-by-four. The driver of the truck jumped out of the cab, clapping Simon on the shoulder, grinning ear to ear. Simon shook his hand and thanked him.

After a few moments, Simon sidled up to Ella, who stood shivering in the cold, a clean cloth someone had apparently given her wrapped around her left hand. "We need to get you to the hospital," he said.

"No. I don't have time for that," she said. "My husband. Where is he?"

"After he saw you fall, he drove off. The attacker went after him."

"Could you tell what direction they went?"

"North. Why?"

"Because we have to follow. The man with the beard was trying to kill Carl."

"I know. But you need attention. There's your head and the—"

He stopped a microsecond before saying the word *baby* and mumbled, "The cut on your hand to consider."

"No, please, you've helped me this much. Can't you help me just a little longer? Take me to the next town. I'll rent a car."

He wasn't sure it would be smart to admit he'd been spying on her, that he knew she had to get to Tampoo. Feeling his way, he said, "Is your memory back, Ella?"

She narrowed her eyes. "Why do you call me Ella? Carl calls me Eleanor."

"Well, I—"

She shook her head impatiently, wincing as her eyes refocused. "Never mind. It doesn't matter. No, my memory hasn't come back, but I now know I have a father who needs me. Something is happening that includes him, something Carl knows more about than he'll tell me. I have to find Carl. I have to get to Washington."

"The police," he said firmly. "They can put an APB out on your rental."

"No police!"

"But they can—"

"No," she insisted. "I don't want the police."

"Why?"

"I don't know," she said, biting her lip. "Just promise, no police."

"I don't—"

"Listen, whatever my father is involved in is dangerous for him and apparently for Carl, too. Carl has a cell phone. If he wants to call the cops, let him."

"Okay, okay, calm down."

"Can't we just drive north to the next town and see if Carl is there?"

Still he paused. Going about this on their own on the heels of that knife attack seemed foolhardy to him. But what about Ella? How deeply was she involved in all this? What had she done that she couldn't remember? He knew she didn't like police work, she'd complained about his job constantly, but without her memory, what was driving her to react to this extreme?

"Yes, okay, I'll help you," he said as though there'd ever been any real doubt he would.

She took a deep breath. Her hands shook as she ran them through her hair.

She began thanking their benefactors. Simon

picked up his green cap from where he'd flung it. Nearby, a woman and her children seemed to be searching for the contents of Ella's spilled handbag and pressing it back into her uninjured hand.

As they left the parking lot, Simon heard sirens approaching from the other direction. It appeared someone had called the fire department to come to the rescue.

"So, why *do* you call me Ella?"

The road they traveled ran high above the ocean with hairpin curves and trees everywhere. Most of the scenery was obscured by the fog. She looked over at him and saw his brows knit.

"My mother's name is Eleanor. Everyone calls her Ella. I guess when I saw you fall I just switched back into an old habit."

"Oh." Well, that kind of made sense. She could see how that could happen. "I'm very lucky you saw me go over that cliff," she added.

"I'd just driven up to the restaurant," he said, "and noticed your husband and the big guy fighting. And then I saw you backing up to escape them."

"You yelled a warning. You yelled Ella."

"Yeah."

"And then you ran toward me."

"I didn't think you saw or heard me," he said,

glancing at her and away as a big camper whizzed by going the other direction.

"I did but kind of in a hazy way. I was just so worried about that damn knife. And Carl had a gun. I didn't know before that he…" Her gaze swiveled to him. "You had a gun, too! I glimpsed it in your hand."

"Yes," he said.

"Why do you carry a gun?"

"I don't know if that's any of your business," he said, but his voice was gentle.

He had a point. Why was she grilling him? Why was she treating him as though she had the right to question anything he did?

He broke the awkward silence by adding, "Would you rather I call you Eleanor?"

"No," she said at once. "I prefer Ella."

"Then Ella it is."

"It was very brave of you to come after me like you did. You saved my life. Thank you."

"You're welcome."

"Are you a fireman?"

"Why would you—oh, because of the rescue?"

"Yes. You know all about ropes. It just seems like the kind of stuff a fireman knows. Don't they rescue people all the time?"

"Mainly we put out fires," he said.

"So you are a fireman," she said. "I was right."

That explained the muscles she'd felt under his clothes as she slid down his body and the way he'd balanced her weight as they scaled the mountain.

"I'm used to helping people out of jams," he added.

"Let's get something straight," she said firmly. "I'm not expecting anything from you but a ride to a car rental place."

"I understand."

"I have to find Carl. He's been lying to me."

"Aren't you worried the guy with the knife will catch up with him first?"

It was her turn for evasion. Worried? Hell yes, if it meant he carved Carl into little pieces. She wanted to ask Carl about her father; she didn't want to find him dead.

Good heavens, was she really such a cold person that she could think like this about a man who claimed they had a good marriage? Yeah, well, he lied; he'd proven that this morning.

The silence was growing and, given the paucity of comforting thoughts in her brain, she blurted out, "You missed breakfast when you rescued me and then I dragged you away."

"I'll grab something later. Actually, I seldom eat before noon."

"My dad was like that. Just coffee with cream. I'd sit in his lap and he'd give me sips."

The words had left her mouth before she realized the significance of the thought behind them—or maybe a more accurate thing to say would be the lack of thought behind them.

Simon pulled the truck off the road into a lookout and set the warning lights. "You remember your father?" His voice sounded excited.

"Not really," she said slowly. "I just suddenly remembered sitting on his lap, drinking his coffee, liking the cream."

But there was more. The warmth of his arm around her waist as he held her, the faint odor of pipe tobacco, his deep voice booming above her head as she took tiny, sweet sips.

Already the memory, so tangible just a second before, began slipping away.

"That's great," Simon said. Hooking one strong arm over the steering wheel, he added, "We need to be honest with each other, not hold things back, don't you agree?"

"Yes," she said quietly, meeting his gaze. For a second, she was back in his arms, hanging from the rope. She'd been frightened, yes, but she'd also felt safe. She added, "I should tell you about the man in the restaurant. But couldn't you drive while I did?"

He blinked a couple of times. "The man in the restaurant?"

"This will all make more sense if you know about him." She motioned with her fingers. "Drive?"

He stared at her a second longer. "Okay," he finally said, and within a few moments, he had merged back into traffic.

She told him about the old guy and the way he'd contrived to meet with her alone and her conviction that Carl had known about the meeting days before. Simon asked if she was sure the old man didn't seem familiar in some way, and though she had to admit he'd appeared to be acquainted with her family, she had no idea who he was or who the man he'd called Jerry was, the man he'd said she was the last to see, presumably before she lost her memory.

They passed a sign announcing the next town a mile away. "So you can see why I need to get to Tampoo, Washington, can't you? I don't know what's going on, but it must be serious. My father needs me. And Carl—he knows something he's not telling."

Simon slowed down as they entered the city. To Ella's dismay it was bigger than Rocky Point. "I'll never find Carl here," she said.

"No, I don't think you will," Simon agreed.

"I thought I'd see our car, but there are hundreds of cars."

"If he has someone on his tail, he won't just pull over."

"And the last time he saw me I was flying off a cliff. He probably thinks I'm dead." She met Simon's gaze and swallowed. If not for him, she would have wound up on the beach a long, long ways down.

Finding Carl was impossible, that was clear to her now, whereas it hadn't been minutes earlier. What else was she missing? Was her light-headed wooziness her natural state of being or was it the result of the concussion?

As she stewed in her own inadequacies, Simon pulled into a grocery store parking lot.

"What are you doing?"

After he'd switched off the engine, he turned to face her again. "Do you agree it's pointless to try to find Carl in this city?"

"Yes. But Tampoo is in Washington and I need a rental."

"Okay, okay, just hear me out. Your eyes look spacey and you have a gash on your hand and Tampoo is easily reached in twenty-four hours. In fact, it will take a lot less than half of that, more like seven or eight. So I'm going to go into this store and buy what it takes to clean and dress your hand and you're going to go into the bathroom and strip off your clothes and wash up whatever got scraped and dirty and make sure you aren't cut and bleeding, um, anywhere important."

"Simon, really."

"It's this or the hospital."

"That's pretty heavy-handed," she said.

"I'm the cautious type. Does your stomach hurt?"

"No. Why would my stomach hurt?"

"You had a concussion," he said. "Nausea and, oh, cramps, maybe, can be a side effect." He looked decidedly uncomfortable as he added, "I just thought the fall might have exacerbated any…conditions."

"I feel queasy every morning. I think it's the medicine I take at night. Anyway, I'll do as you ask."

"You will?"

"It makes sense to me. You act surprised."

He shrugged. "The last woman I was close to wasn't quite as agreeable as you are."

"Is this the one you were telling me about last night?"

"Yes."

"I guess I'm just the easygoing type."

His smile seemed wistful to her and she wondered how long ago he'd broken up with this woman. Maybe the wound was still raw. That thought seemed to rekindle the throbbing in her left hand and she glanced down. What caught her eye was the slender band of gold on her ring finger, a band tying her to Carl.

Had he left her to die on the cliff or had his motive for leaving been to lead the man with the knife away from her? If so, that posed the question—what kind of loyalty did she owe Carl? Should she believe him when he claimed they had a good marriage? Were her current misgivings out of place? When she saw him again—and there wasn't a doubt in her mind he would show up in Tampoo unless the guy with the knife stopped him—should she give him the benefit of the doubt? He was her husband, after all....

She remembered the chill that raced through her blood when he touched her....

And the lies. He'd known about that meeting at the restaurant and now he knew about the one in Tampoo. What if Carl represented the threat to her father? She might not remember him to speak of, but she'd had one searing moment of clarity and this she knew—she loved her father. She would do anything for him.

"You okay?" Simon said.

"What? Oh, sure."

"You look upset."

"I guess I am."

"It'll all work out," he said softly, then shook his head and added, "I sound like a greeting card."

"You know, I still don't know your last name."

"Task."

"And I'm Ella Baxter. I can't remember if I told you my last name before."

"Pleased to formally meet you," he said, taking her right hand in his. The touch of his skin sent a million fireflies dancing up her arm.

"Let's get this over with," she said, withdrawing her hand and steeling herself for the moment Simon would drop her off at the car rental place and go his own way. The moment she would be alone except for the fleeting images of a faceless father who had given her sips of coffee some twenty-odd years before.

Chapter Five

So, now he'd lied to her.

Repeatedly.

Simon put bandages, ointments and other supplies in a shopping basket before retracing his steps to the front of the store, where he waited near the alcove that led to the supermarket restrooms. His concern was that besides scrapes and bruises and the gash in her hand, the fall had caused Ella to miscarry her baby.

Was her baby his baby? They'd been together at the time she must have gotten pregnant, but he couldn't swear that she hadn't been seeing Carl Baxter, too. He found it hard—and distressful—to think she would sleep with another man when he and she were lovers, but there was that secret side of Ella he had to consider, the side that led to her compartmentalizing her life so that he knew little about what she did when she wasn't with him.

And there was the recent withdrawn behavior, her unwillingness to share whatever was troubling her. It had begun a good month before and she'd countered his concerns by telling him being a cop didn't give him the right to butt into her business.

Hadn't loving her given him that right?

How in the world could he tell her she was pregnant and yet how could he keep it from her? And how would he convince her to allow him to come along on her trip to Tampoo and wherever it led next? He absolutely couldn't allow her to go on alone, not after that knife fight.

Did he have time to call home and see if the P.I. he'd called the day before had news or even to call Ginny and see if she'd found out anything from Ella's doctors?

He was about to reach for his cell when Ella appeared in the alcove, limping now, clutching her big handbag to her chest. For the first time he noticed the extent of the scratches on her skin and tears in her clothes. She looked pale and feverish at the same time, the bandage on her head sporting bright red stains as though bleeding anew. They were going to need some gauze.

"You're limping," he said as she drew near.

"I think I twisted an ankle or something. It's no big deal."

"How about other contusions and, er, bleeding?"

"Nothing serious. A few scratches. I think my clothes got the worst of it."

He motioned at her handbag. "I meant to ask if you've checked to see if all your belongings are in there."

"I haven't looked yet." She started to open her purse, then paused as her stomach made a gurgling noise. They both smiled. "Oops, pardon me, I think I'm hungry. It kicks in every day about this time, I guess when the medicine from the night before wears off."

"Let's see if we can find some sandwiches to eat on the run."

"Or maybe some good rolls and a few deli supplies," she said, and he smiled internally. His Ella had not been a fast food or ready-made type of girl. She'd been something of a closet gourmet, more likely to choose French Camembert than Wisconsin cheddar. "Whatever you like," he said.

His mind raced as they walked through the aisles collecting more first aid items and a supply of bottled water on their way to the in-store deli. Would she have told him if she was bleeding in a way that indicated problems with a pregnancy? Maybe not, maybe she'd be shy to mention it, but surely she would have bought herself something to help with bleeding and that would have meant she would have to open her purse and look in her wallet for change. She said she hadn't. No reason for her to lie about that, so he had to trust that, for now, the baby was safe. The thing to do was get Ella off her feet ASAP.

"Look at that," she said, stopping suddenly. She was staring at a display of sweatshirts and sweat-pants, most of them dark-green-and-white and sporting a local high school logo. "I only have a credit card. Do you think the store would accept it?"

"Probably not," he said quickly as an idea flashed through his brain. "I'll get what you want."

"You wouldn't mind?"

"No."

She immediately began digging through the clothes for the right sizes. She'd set her purse in the top of the basket to have her uninjured hand free, and now with her back turned to him, he slid his hand inside the unzipped bag, groped around until his fingers touched what felt like her wallet and quickly extracted it. Bingo. It went in his pocket in a flash. Now she had no driver's license, and without a driver's license, she couldn't rent a car.

"What do you think?" she said. She'd managed to find a pale blue set of sweats and held them against her chest. A small painted dolphin leaped across her breasts.

"You look good in blue," he said softly. He'd always thought so.

There was a chair in the alcove. After they'd paid for everything, he slathered her up with antibiotics and wrapped gauze around her a couple of turns shy of a mummy. She went back into the bathroom and emerged a few minutes later wearing the blue sweats.

"I wonder if the real me would be as horrified by this getup as the current me is," she mused, putting her old clothes in an empty paper bag.

"I think you look kind of cute. Sporty."

"Let's go find a rental place, okay? I want to cross the state line into Washington tonight, and I'm sure you have a life to get back to."

"Absolutely," he said, "although the fact is, I'm on a few days' leave right now. That's how firemen in my area work. A day on, a day off, eventually four days off…it's called a tour and it leaves discretionary time." And that was true of the Blue Mountain Fire Department. It just wasn't true of him, though a call for time off had taken care of that problem with the Blue Mountain Police Department.

The next hour or so played out as he knew it would, although he felt crummy lying to her again. Once she found her wallet was missing, she insisted they call the credit card company until she realized she didn't know the name of the company or even remember what kind of card it was. As he knew it was safe in his pocket, he told her they'd worry about it when they stopped for the night. Between now and then, he'd have to figure out a way to get her wallet back to her.

Being without a valid driver's license had accomplished exactly what it was supposed to—it had kept her from renting a car. She'd accepted his continued help with a weariness suggesting she was just too frazzled to fight it. After she'd fixed them sandwiches from goodies she'd chosen at the deli counter, she'd fallen into a deep sleep, head against the door, cushioned on his jacket.

He glanced at her several times, wishing she'd wake up and be the old Ella, the one with answers instead of questions. True, he found this more open version of Ella very appealing in her way. She had all the wit and charm and beguiling oddities of the original woman without the wariness that had ultimately driven them apart.

What had she done that had put her in this position? He'd be willing to bet it had started when they were still together. The way she'd left her house, her odd haircut and color—and where in the hell had Carl Baxter come from? What did he have to do with Ella's father?

For that matter, how did they know this was really about Ella's father? The only time she'd mentioned family to him was to tell him they were all dead. Now, just because some old guy fed her a line, he was supposed to believe there was a whole secret plot going on? On the other hand, Carl Baxter and the big guy with a knife were absolutely real….

Bottom line: Was Ella in danger or was someone else in danger because of her?

He needed to get somewhere private and make a few phone calls.

ELLA WOKE UP as Simon pulled into another parking lot, this one belonging to a sprawling motel. The fact that it was already dark meant she'd slept for hours.

"Where are we?" she asked after a yawn that seemed to crack her face. She was stiff, sore, headachy and hurt just about everywhere.

"We're a hundred or so miles south of Tampoo. I'm too tired to drive any more. We can easily travel the rest of the way tomorrow morning."

She didn't argue. She wasn't the one putting in the hours behind the wheel.

"I chose a one-story motel," he explained as they got out of the truck, "just to be on the safe side."

"The safe side of what?"

"I just like having my feet close to the ground. You know, in case."

She let it drop. Maybe it was a fireman thing.

He checked them in as Mr. and Mrs. Simon Task, a fact she also didn't dispute. The man was paying for everything—she hoped she had enough money somewhere to reimburse him. If he wanted them both in one room, that was fine with her.

They immediately walked across the parking lot to the restaurant next door and ordered dinner.

"How do you do it?" Simon asked, sitting back in his chair and gazing at her across the table. His gray eyes were full of warmth and speculation and she found herself patting at her hair, wishing she'd thought to buy a comb.

"How do I do what?"

"Order food. How do you know you like morel risotto?"

"How do I know anything?" she mused. "It's a mystery to me, too. I mean, if I can figure out what I like to eat, why can't I figure out who I am?"

"Today you remembered a detail about your father. Have you remembered anything else?"

"I had a dream about him this afternoon. I was riding in the back of a black pickup truck, sitting on a dragon. Well, not really a dragon, one of those floaty things that blow up, the kind kids play with."

"How old were you?"

"I don't know. Little, I think. There was a boy sitting next to me dressed like Tarzan. He had a toy gun."

Simon chuckled. "Where does your father come into this?"

"The boy turned into my father. One minute he was a kid with a red water pistol and the next he was my father and he was holding me in his lap and telling me it was dangerous to ride in the back of a truck but that he would protect me."

"Did you see his face? How did you know it was your dad?"

"No face. I just knew." Her eyes burned as she smiled at herself. "Crazy, huh?"

"It sounds as if you're close to your father."

"I know I am, I just know it. Oh, Simon, promise me you'll help me get to him. He needs help, I know he does. If I fail him I'll never forgive myself."

He narrowed his eyes.

"Promise," she said, uncertain why she was demanding this near stranger make such a pledge.

"I'll do what I can," he said.

"You must think I'm crazy."

"No," he said thoughtfully. "I think you're a woman with one person you can remember and I think he means the world to you."

"You do understand. I keep thinking about Carl. I'm sure he was using me to get to my father. What if Carl's goal is to hurt Dad? He had a gun, you know."

"The big guy with the knife kicked Carl's gun down into the ocean."

"But maybe Carl will buy another one. Why didn't I have the presence of mind to ask the old guy at the restaurant a few questions?"

"Probably because you didn't know what he was talking about. Go easy on yourself."

"Maybe we should have kept driving."

"Even if we drove all night, we can't do anything until tomorrow at noon, right?"

"Yes. Right."

They fell silent as salads were delivered. Ella noticed the waitress gave her a double take and wondered if additional bruises had blossomed on her face since the fall. Maybe it was better not to know.

Despite her nerves and the near silence they fell into as they ate, Ella enjoyed the meal more than any she could recall since waking with amnesia five days before. It wasn't just the food, either, it was the company, and perhaps it wasn't even the fact that Simon sat across from her as much as it was that Carl didn't.

He gives me the creeps, she thought.

"What?"

She'd spoken it aloud. She said, "Carl. I didn't like the look in his eyes."

"What do you mean?"

"He always looked as though he was laughing at me, inside, you know?"

"Very unpleasant."

"Creepy. Nice way for a wife to feel about her husband, isn't it?"

"You said you saw his driver's license."

"Yes."

"The same last name might mean he's your brother or an ex-husband, you know."

The thought Carl Baxter could be a blood relative made her queasy and she set aside her fork. "Not a brother," she said firmly. "The old man said my brother was dead."

"Then an ex-husband."

"Maybe. There's no denying the man knows things about me. I mean little things a man who didn't live with a woman wouldn't know."

"Such as?"

"Such as I have a mole on my, er, abdomen and another one on my breasts, neither in places people would normally see. And he knew about them."

"Intimate places," Simon said with a slow smile.

"Yes."

"How did he pay for your hospital stay?"

"I don't know. He told me not to worry about things like that. It makes me wonder if I'm always compliant."

He took a bite of his steak and shrugged.

"I keep wondering where I met Carl. I mean, I must know him in some capacity for our names to be the same. I just can't imagine myself being attracted to him. Maybe he's a long-lost third cousin once removed, but then why did he pretend to be my husband?"

Simon folded his napkin and sat back in his chair. "Good point."

"Tell me how you met her."

"How I met who?"

"The girl you broke up with. Tell me how you met."

His eyes took on a faraway look, though he didn't avert his gaze. "It was at a dance," he said slowly. "A masquerade dance I got talked into attending with a buddy of mine. I went as a pirate because I had an eye patch left over from something."

"And she was there?"

"She came as a mermaid. She had very long hair and it flowed all around her shoulders and down her back and she was wearing all this blue and green like the water. Every square inch of her seemed to shimmer when she moved."

"It sounds beautiful."

"It was. She was. She had on a mask so I couldn't see all of her face, just her eyes, but I knew she was it."

"She was the one."

"She was like a free spirit that night."

"You make it sound like she changed."

"She did, but that came later. I'll always have that night, I'll always remember the woman I met at the party."

She laid her napkin across the plate. "You loved her."

"I did."

"So how did it end?"

"I guess you could say I left her."

She tilted her head slightly as she looked at him. "But you still have feelings for her."

His gaze sharpened. "That's true, I do. She wasn't the kind of woman a man forgets overnight."

"Maybe there's hope you can get back together," she said. Had anyone ever loved her that way? Had Carl? Was he even capable of that kind of love? Was she?

"It's getting late," Simon finally said.

While he went back to his truck to get his luggage and the first-aid supplies in case anything needed redressing, Ella went into a small variety-type store with Simon's credit card in hand. There wasn't a lot to choose from, but she did find something to sleep in. They walked down the hall wrapped in their own thoughts.

Ella felt nervous about being alone in a room whose most obvious piece of furniture was a bed, but she told herself to grow up. If she could handle being close to Carl for several days, she could handle one night with Simon. At least she *liked* Simon.

"Why don't you use the bathroom first and then I'll take a shower?" he told her.

She pulled the knee-length sleeping shirt from the gift-shop bag and went into the bathroom, where a cursory look in the mirror revealed a total mess. Even her short hair looked defeated. When it grew out a little, she'd get herself to a decent beauty shop. This cut appeared to have been done by someone with their eyes shut.

A few minutes later, she walked into the bedroom to find Simon sitting in a chair next to a small round table. He looked up at her, his gaze flicking down her body as though he couldn't help himself. She saw all sorts of things flash in his eyes, things that made her insides sizzle. The T-shirt material suddenly seemed very, very thin.

"You're not limping anymore," he said.

"No, my ankle doesn't hurt."

"Are you finished in there?"

"It's all yours." He got to his feet in one fluid motion, reminding her again of the way he'd clasped her to his side on the mountain, the strength in his arms. As six feet of potent masculinity walked toward her, she had to remind herself to breathe.

Simon paused a step away from her. "Do you need help rebandaging anything?"

"No," she said, craning her neck back to look up at him. Their posture was perfect for embracing, for kissing; it was only the foot of space between them that sounded an off note. The hammering heartbeat, the flushed skin, the super-sexual awareness—that was all there in spades, and unless she was even more clueless than she thought she was, it was there for him, too.

"I'll be a few minutes," he said as he went into the bathroom.

SIMON GAVE HIMSELF a stern lecture about poorly timed hormone attacks as he turned on the shower to cover the sound of his voice. He sat on the closed commode and punched in the number for the P.I. back in Blue Mountain.

"I thought you'd never call back," Devin Kittimer said as soon as he heard Simon's voice. Devin was a decade older than Simon, but a job at Devin's office one summer had been the deciding factor in Simon going to the police academy.

"It's been a little busy on my end. Did you find out anything about Carl Baxter?"

"He was born in Chicago forty-one years ago. Only child, parents alive but separated. Married Eleanor Thorton a few days after her eighteenth birthday when he was in his mid-thirties. The marriage lasted nine weeks before the split. There's some question about the legality of the divorce. Anyway, she apparently moved around quite a bit until ending up in Blue Mountain. She probably told you all this a year ago when you guys got together."

Simon was embarrassed to admit she'd never said one word about any of it. Not a single word. Why had she worked so hard to bury her past?

At any rate, it now appeared Carl Baxter was either her ex-husband or a husband she'd thought she'd left behind. It seemed unlikely Ella was carrying his baby.

Unless he'd come to town and won her back....

"What about Ella?" he said. "Did you call the radio station like I asked?"

"Yes. They have no idea where she is. Her boss was getting worried about her, in fact."

"So she left without telling them."

"I gave the guy some song and dance about a sick relative, and then I went by Ella's house and spoke to a few of her neighbors. Other than the fact that they noticed her house was lit up in the middle of the night, no one had wondered too much about not seeing her. I gather she often worked late hours and spent her free time in the backyard, gardening. No one saw anything suspicious around the time she apparently left."

"So, it wasn't a planned trip or she would have spoken to her boss."

"And stopped her newspaper, which she didn't. Other than that, the years before she got married are hard to figure. I have a few calls out, should know more tomorrow.

"Oh, one thing, Carl Baxter has a rap sheet a mile long. Mostly B and E when he was a kid, some con man stuff, bad checks, things like that. Got a little more inventive as he got older. Was part of a street gang running juice loans in Chicago. Car theft, et cetera. Did time in Tallahassee Road Prison down in Florida, been out a few months. He's also had a few aliases. Carl Stickler, Jay Mornajay, William Smith to name a few."

"Great," Simon said, running a hand through his hair. "You'll keep digging on Ella for me? Find out about her parents, if you can, especially her father."

"Sure."

"Thanks, Devin."

"No problem."

Simon's next call was to his cousin Virginia, who sounded as though he'd woken her up. She mumbled she hadn't been able to find anyone who knew anyone else at the hospital where Ella had been treated and a call to the attending physician had not yet been returned.

"I'm not sure how much he'll tell me even if he does call back," Ginny cautioned.

After hearing details of what had happened to Ella that day, she added, "This sounds increasingly dangerous, coz. I'm not sure you should allow her to continue this search."

Allow her? What a concept! Virginia obviously thought he had more control than he did. "She's determined to find her father. She had a spontaneous memory of him today and dreamed about him, too."

"Positive stuff?"

"Very. She obviously adores him. She's very anxious to find him."

"I wonder why she never told you about him."

"You and me both."

"But this is exactly why you should continue to protect her from too much truth. Her memory is coming back on its own."

"Following a knife fight and a long drop down a cliff," he reminded her.

"True. Still, play it close to the vest, give her another few days."

He'd known that was coming, but he'd hoped she'd tell him to spill his guts. "Okay."

"Call back tomorrow and stay away from steep cliffs and thugs with knives."

"That's my plan."

"You sound bushed. Go to bed."

He clicked off his phone, undressed and showered. He was too tired to shave and it wasn't as though he was going to kiss anyone anyway.

For a second, he was overcome with the not so distant memory of Ella running her fingers along his jaw while nibbling on his earlobe, whispering what they could do if he wanted to take a few minutes and shave—

He splashed cold water on his face. The Ella that memory belonged to was gone; those times were gone. If she was pregnant with his child, they'd have to figure out a way to parent together, but they couldn't be together; they'd tried and failed and he'd be wise to remember that. The excited gleam in her eye when she looked at him now made his groin ache with want, but he knew it would fizzle out and die the moment she remembered their shared past.

He let himself back into the room while holding a towel around his waist. He normally slept nude but not tonight. He'd just forgotten to take clean clothes into the bathroom with him.

He'd been away so long, he was pretty sure she'd be asleep. The lights were dimmed and he took a few steps toward his duffel before he realized she wasn't in the bed; she was sitting on a chair by the small table in the corner. Her face was deep in shadows, though he could see the glistening whites of her eyes as she stared at him.

And then he saw what lay on the table in front of her.

Chapter Six

Holding the towel in place, Simon sat down on the edge of the bed, facing her. Gesturing at the table, he said, "You found my badge?"

"I saw the leather folder sitting in your open bag. I was curious so I looked."

"It's okay," he said.

"My snooping or your lying? Which do you mean? Which is okay?"

"Now, wait a second—"

"Are you going to try to explain why you told me you were a fireman?"

"I guess I'd better."

"Make it good," she said, and there was a deadly earnestness to her voice he'd heard before. This was the Ella from before the amnesia, the woman whose middle name was suspicion.

"Do you remember this morning when I suggested we call the police to help Carl and you wouldn't let me?"

"Yes."

"It wasn't ten minutes later that you assumed I was a fireman. It was obvious to me that you had a thing about cops."

"So you lied."

"You were shaken and upset and I didn't know how long we'd be in each other's company at that point, so I let you reach your own conclusions and went along with them. In other words, yes, I lied and for that I'm sorry."

She picked up the badge, ran her fingers over the surface and his heart sank. He'd completely zoned out on the fact that Blue Mountain was engraved on the badge.

"Now tell me why you never told me we come from the same town. It's quite a coincidence, isn't it?"

"What do you mean?" he said, taking the defensive. He didn't have time to review every last one of their conversations, but he was pretty sure he was on safe ground. "Are you from Blue Mountain, too?"

"You know I am," she said.

"How would I know that?"

"I'm sure I mentioned it."

"Nope."

"Are you trying to tell me it's just a coincidence

we meet hundreds of miles from home and we come from the same place?"

"Why not?" he said. "Stranger things have happened."

She got up from the chair and walked over to him, the badge still in her hand. He prepared himself to have it lobbed at his chest, but she shocked the hell out of him by gently handing it over.

"I wish I didn't know you were a cop," she said.

Not what he expected. He said, "What does it matter?"

"I don't like cops. I don't trust them."

"Please believe me, I have nothing but your best interest at heart. Honest."

"Just tell me this. Are you the reason the thought of the police getting involved in my life makes me want to run for the hills?"

"No," he said, and that was the truth. Whatever had caused her to panic at the thought of police had started way before him. His job had been a bone of contention between them from the moment she found out about it.

Why was it such a big deal to her? It had never made sense to him and it didn't make sense now. Unless she had a record of some kind, unless she was on the run….

"Are you after Carl? Are you after my father? Are you using me to get to him the way Carl was?"

"Absolutely not."

"Are you here because you're a cop?"

"No. I'm here in this room at this moment helping you because of you. Period."

"Why?"

"Because you need help."

"And you spend your off time looking for damsels in distress?"

"Not usually, no. For you, I made an exception."

"Why?"

"You know why," he said.

"I don't know anything, remember?"

He took a step toward her and held on to her shoulders, resisting the habit of pulling her into a full embrace. She'd always fit against him perfectly. She was exactly the right height, exactly the right shape, her body a perfect match for his.

If it was just that easy.

"It started in the lobby when we exchanged our first words, when I touched your wedding band," he said softly. "I felt you tremble. The next day when I saw you disappear over a mountainside, what was I supposed to do, look the other way?"

She cocked her head. The bathroom light spilled across her cheekbones. Between the bandages and the short, dark hair, she almost looked like a stranger.

"Why do I want to trust you so much?" she said softly.

"Because somewhere in your heart you know you can."

"You could be part of this."

"But I'm not."

She blinked quickly. Her beautiful face was scratched and black-and-blue, bandaged, scraped, but there was nothing wrong with her lips. They were as luscious as ever. He knew she wouldn't stop him if he bent his head and…

And when her memory came back and she recalled the last night they had spent together, the things he'd said to her, the things she'd said to him, the past that lay between them? What then?

He dropped his hands from her shoulders, making sure the towel stayed in place around his waist. "Let's hit the sack," he said.

She mumbled, "I could use a stiff drink."

So could he. But if she couldn't drink, he wouldn't drink. There was a baby between them, too, and his gaze dipped to her midsection, where he thought he could detect a new curve against the cotton of her gown.

"Sleep will do us both more good," he said, dragging his gaze back to her face. "Maybe tomorrow this will all make sense."

Grabbing his duffel, he changed into clean boxers and a T-shirt in the bathroom. When he returned to the room, he found she'd tucked herself under the sheets. It was obvious she needed sleep. He, on the other hand, had some serious thinking to do. Knowing he'd be out like a light if he darkened the room, he left the lamp burning and settled back against the headboard.

"ELLA? ELLA, WAKE UP."

Though his voice was a whisper, the urgency in it cut through her sleep like a bullhorn, shattering a dream. Her eyes flew open.

Simon was sitting on the bed beside her, his body tense. As she met his gaze, his finger pressed against her lips and he motioned with his head toward the door.

She heard a very subtle rattle and then the knob slowly turned. She would have gasped but for the presence of Simon's warning finger.

She met his gaze and he lowered his head to whisper in her ear. "It may be nothing but some drunk trying to get in the wrong room. I'm going out the bathroom window. Lock it behind me."

"Why are you going to do that?" she whispered back.

"I want to know who it is," he said as though it was reasonable.

"We could just open the door—"

"Are you forgetting this morning?"

The gash in her hand seemed to spring into

flames. No, she wasn't forgetting, but she wanted to beg Simon to stay. She didn't want to be alone and she was afraid for him. "Okay," she said, working to make sure her voice didn't betray her fears, though those fears were clawing their way up her throat.

Simon quietly slipped off the bed. He pulled on his jeans and shoes, stuck his gun in his waist holster. She followed him into the bathroom, closing the door behind them so light from the bedroom wouldn't illuminate the window over the bathtub.

"Don't open the door for anyone," he cautioned as he stepped into the tub. "Make sure the chain is engaged."

"No kidding."

He slid the glass panel back and popped off the screen. All that was visible from Ella's point of view was a tall overhead mercury vapor lamp illuminating the side of a nearby building.

It took Simon a moment to twist his body through the narrow opening. When she heard his feet hit the pavement outside, she closed the window behind him and relocked it. Back in the bedroom, she double-checked the door before changing back into her blue sweat suit and shoes. When she heard another rattle at the door, she tiptoed across the room, waiting for a signal that it was Simon. Why hadn't they agreed on some kind of code knock? She stood so close to the wood panel the warmth of her breath bounced back on her face. If anything, her heart pounded harder than it had when she'd been caught on that tree, dangling above the ocean.

Who was out there?

The knob turned.

SIMON RAN AROUND THE PERIMETER of the motel, searching for a doorway back into the building. The only one he found was marked Hotel Personnel and was locked. He had to go all the way back to the lobby to reenter and then make his way cautiously back down the hallway.

The space in front of their door was empty, but he caught a glimpse of a man turning a corner into another corridor several yards beyond it. Staying close to the outside wall, he hurried along, peeking around the corner in time to see the same man push open the doors emptying out into the courtyard pool area.

He'd seen the man that very morning, wearing the same black clothes.

Obviously, the man with the knife had waited somewhere along the way and followed Simon and Ella to this motel. Had he dispatched Carl and was he now hunting Ella? Maybe he'd been trying to kill Carl to get to her that morning.

The questions were immaterial. Whatever this man knew, Simon needed to know. He had to get the jump on him; if Ella was in trouble with the law, so be it. He couldn't protect her forever if she'd done something terrible, and the sooner it was out in the open, the better. If Carl was dead, which seemed a likely scenario given the big man's presence at the motel, then it became even more important to make him talk.

Giving the guy a few seconds to get away from the doors, Simon practically slithered around the corner. He peered through the glass inset in the door and saw the big man standing with his back to the motel.

How to get out the door without drawing attention? When he heard raised voices, he realized there must be someone out there with him. The odds had just shifted. Nevertheless, the noise of the argument might cover the sound of him opening the door.

He took a deep breath and pushed on the glass, sliding out and into the shadows as fast as he could. The first place he found shelter was behind an electrical power unit that emitted a hum. As handy as it was for concealment, it was too noisy for eavesdropping.

Another peek revealed the men still talking, but they'd lowered their voices even more as though aware a shouting match after midnight would draw attention. Simon kept low as he moved behind a handy clump of bushes and on to an equipment locker.

It was time to decide what to do. As a police officer in Oregon, he was on duty 24/7, but he wasn't acting much like a police officer right now. He could arrest the big guy for attacking Carl Baxter, and Ella could verify she'd seen the fight, but without Carl around to prosecute, how far would that go?

Of course, if Carl showed up dead, it would be a whole other matter.

Bottom line: if he used his official standing to try to get the big guy to open up, then he'd also have to be willing to hand Ella over to the authorities if that was appropriate. He needed a nonconfrontational way in which to get the man to talk.

He snuck another look, and this time the big man was pacing, obviously frustrated, grumbling as he walked, his voice spiking every few seconds. The other man suddenly stood up and moved into the light, grabbing the big guy's shoulder, spinning him around to face him, his back still to Simon. The two men jabbed at each other's chests, their voices still subdued, but loud enough for Simon to finally get the gist of the problem.

They were arguing about whether they should

break down a door and take what they wanted. The big guy was in favor of waiting until morning. He'd tried the door; it was locked; a break-in would just create a scene. The other man said he could get in the room without detection, no problem, he'd done it before. He didn't want to wait until daylight; too much might go wrong.

There was little doubt in Simon's mind which door they were talking about and who they wanted to get their hands on.

The smaller man turned around.

Simon blinked a few times, his brain trying to assimilate what he saw and what it meant.

Carl Baxter.

The only reason he'd be here was if he'd joined forces with his adversary way back this morning. The two of them had to be working together, but why the fight, what was the purpose?

Wait, hold on, who cared? The reasons for everything could wait. What he needed right now were answers, and there were the two men who could fill in all the gaps, ripe for the plucking, only twenty feet away. Okay, they were both undoubtedly armed seeing as they were willing to enter a motel room where they must know Simon slept along with Ella. Surely they'd seen his gun that morning.

Could he take them both?

He felt a vibration in his pocket and ignored it for a minute. Voices lowered, the men started toward the far side of the motel where a parallel wing offered additional rooms. They were either refining their game plan or retreating until morning. How to tell?

He could follow them, maybe trap them in their room if indeed that's where they were headed.

The phone vibrated again. He grabbed it from his pocket and flipped it open to check caller ID. As he did, he heard the bigger man say, "Okay, you win."

That meant tonight….

He hit the button when he saw it was Virginia. Moving swiftly back toward his own door, he took care to stay covered in case the men turned around. "Ginny?" he whispered. "This isn't a good time…."

"I just got a call from that doctor I tried to get a hold of earlier today."

"It's the middle of the night," he said, incredulous.

"He called because when I left a message for him, I mentioned Ella's name. The police had just awoken him. Do you know your little Ella is wanted in connection with a murder back in Blue Mountain?"

"No," he said, his heart sinking. He looked over his shoulder to see both men entering through the far door. He ducked inside his own wing and walked quickly down the hall as he spoke. "Did you tell them I'm with her and where we are?"

"I don't know where you are, coz. You've been very careful to never tell me an exact location, and for that I thank you. But no, I didn't tell him about you, I made up something."

Why hadn't Devin said anything about this when they talked earlier? Murder? "Who's dead?" he asked.

"I don't know. Apparently the dead man was discovered in a vacant lot a couple of days ago, but now the police want to question Ella. I don't have details, I don't know how they knew she was in the accident or the hospital, but the other doctor is bound to tell them I was asking questions."

"Not necessarily, but if they do, tell them the truth, don't perjure yourself. I have to go."

"I want you to listen to reason. This is your career we're talking about—"

"Ginny? Not now. Thanks for the warning."

He snapped the cell closed and tapped on the room door. "Ella? It's me, Simon."

He heard the rattle of the chain and then the door flew open. Ella took a few hasty steps back into the room. "Did you find out who was out there?"

He locked the door behind him, leaving the chain unhooked this time. If the thugs broke into the room, he didn't want management alerted.

Better they should enter and see the room empty and go away.

"We have to leave," he said.

"Why? Who was it? That awful man with the knife?"

He started throwing his things into his bag. "Yeah, it was him, all right, but he's apparently in cahoots with someone else you know. Carl was out there and I think one or the other of them is on his way here."

Her face drained of color. "I thought the guy with the knife tried to kill Carl."

"I did, too."

She shook her head. "Even if they're cohorts now, why not just cut us off tomorrow? Carl knows where we're headed. Wait a second, how did either one of them know we were here in this motel?"

"They must have been trailing us all day," he said, his professional pride taking a hit. He hadn't detected a tail. He'd never even really thought to look for one. He stuffed Ella's few belongings into the gift shop bag. "Anything else?" he said, looking around.

"But that man tried to kill Carl."

"Unless it was staged."

"Why would they stage—"

"I don't know," he snapped, then took a deep breath. "I don't know," he said more calmly.

meeting her gaze. "Maybe they had a falling-out, maybe the big guy caught up with Carl and they decided to go in together, I just don't know."

"They're coming after me," she said, her eyes growing hard. Every once in a while the old Ella showed up, and this time, he welcomed her arrival. "Just let them come," she said. "You have a gun, you're a damn policeman, right?"

"What about your father?"

Her lashes fluttered against her cheeks. "You're right, we can't risk my not getting to Tampoo, can we?"

"No. That's why we're going out the bathroom window."

Without another word, she turned on her heel and made for the bathroom. He unlocked the window again and slid it open, then threw their belongings outside. Since the drop to the ground was the more difficult part of the escape, Simon went first. Ella managed to get herself through the opening and more or less dropped into his arms, crying out softly when he grabbed her. No doubt he'd touched her hand or one of the other abrasions she'd suffered.

"Where's the truck?" she asked, looking around the parking area, trying to orientate herself.

"Out front." He'd been worrying about this since the moment he knew they had to leave. If he were trying to trap someone, he'd send one man to the room and the other to guard the getaway vehicle. Therefore, the best thing to do was abandon the truck.

But he'd signed into this motel using his real name and giving his license number, so it wouldn't be long before the motel would either tow the truck or have it impounded, and Ella's wallet was on the passenger-side floor under the seat where he'd put it a few hours before. If things ever got linked together, this would put her in his company.

All this meant it was time to take sides. He was either a lawman or a man dedicated to helping Eleanor Baxter figure things out. A man willing to risk everything for a woman who was probably carrying his baby or a man who threw her to the mercy of the court with the hope she actually wasn't involved in a murder.

No way. He did not want his baby born in prison and sometimes, as much as he hated to admit it, the law got things wrong.

Or had he got things wrong? Was it possible she carried another man's child? "We're walking," he grumbled.

"All the way to Tampoo?"

"It's coming up on closing time at the bars."

"*Now* you want a drink?" she said, her limp reappearing.

"Stay close to the side of the building," he cautioned as he pulled her onto the darker half of the sidewalk. "It won't take them long to figure out we're gone. I have a feeling the stakes are higher than either one of us can guess."

She fell silent beside him, her breathing growing strained as he hurried her along.

What had happened to make two men hell-bent on murdering each other this morning join forces now?

One thing was certain. Carl was no doubt at that moment storming their room, risking detection and possible arrest if hotel management got wind of things. That was the act of a reckless man.

And a reckless man was a deadly man.

Chapter Seven

Ella soon discovered closing time at a bar was a great place to catch a taxi. Simon gave directions to head for the nearest town to the north with a bus station.

"There's a depot right here in Witchit, buddy," the driver announced.

"I don't want this one," Simon insisted.

"It's your dime," the driver said, "but just so you know, the next town is about twelve dark miles from here."

"That's fine."

Ella was seated very close to Simon, more or less in the same spot she'd landed upon getting into the cab, too tired and frightened to seek distance. "That's our plan? We're taking a bus to Tampoo?"

The light was spare inside the cab, reducing Simon to a shape darker than the shadows around him. He pulled her into his arms and spoke into her ear, his voice a whisper. "Not all the way to

Tampoo. Too dangerous. We'll get off short of the place, rent a car and drive so we're not stuck when we get there."

"Good, because the last time we met with one of my father's contacts, I went off a cliff."

"Exactly."

They were silent for the rest of the ride. Simon paid the driver when he let them off, and though it occurred to Ella that he was going exceptionally far out of his way to help her, she let it go. Time would reveal his real motives; for now she had to trust what he'd told her—he was with her because she needed him. There was absolutely no denying that fact.

"Bus straight through to Seattle leaves at 6:00 a.m.," the depot manager announced.

"Too long a wait out in the open," Simon muttered, looking around the deserted building in such a way that Ella shuddered. She expected Carl and the man with the knife to burst through the doors at any moment.

"There's a puddle jumper comes through in about fifteen minutes, but it won't get you there any faster," the manager said, his gaze lingering on Ella's bandages.

"Did it stop in Witchit?"

"Yeah."

"Did it take on passengers?"

"How would I know?"

Simon bought the tickets and the two of them moved into the waiting room. Ella was too anxious to sit on the old chairs sprinkled about the area despite her weariness. She leaned against the wall instead.

The bus showed up on schedule. Simon shooed her into the restroom. "You're not getting on board until I make sure Carl or the big guy isn't on that bus."

"Why would they be on the bus?"

"If they figured out how we might leave town without our vehicle, one of them could be on board. I'll knock on the door, okay?"

She did as he asked. Every minute of the five-minute wait seemed to take an hour before she heard a couple of raps on the door and exited to find Simon standing there. "All clear," he said.

The bus was mostly empty. Simon guided her to the bench seat in the back. Ella sank onto the worn vinyl gratefully, scooting to the corner where she could rest her head. She closed her eyes, aware of Simon stowing his duffel and her bag in the overhead bin but too tired to care about anything.

Besides, maybe if she slept she would dream, maybe she would see her father again. The first time she'd thought of him, she'd been very small, sitting on his lap while he drank coffee. The second time she'd been a few years older and there had been a little boy there, too. The third time was just that night when Simon woke her up and she could remember none of the details, just that her father had been near her.

But sleep wouldn't come. The bus stopped too often, the secondary roads it traveled twisted and curved and she was very aware of Simon looking out the back window as though checking for someone following them.

She thought back the four, no, five days now since she'd woken up in the hospital, looked up at Carl and wondered who he was. In the next instant, it had come as a shock to realize she didn't know who *she* was.

It had been so frightening at first, so odd to hear people talk about her as though they knew her secrets and she did not. She'd been so frustrated at the curtain of silence that surrounded her, reinforced by Carl. She'd accepted his word that the doctors wanted her kept in the dark until her memories came back on their own, but now she realized she couldn't take anything about Carl for granted; everything he'd done or said since she'd met him in the hospital had to be reassessed.

She detected one bright light in the dark cavern of her mind; though her memory was still as full of holes as an old boat sitting on the bottom of a lake, she was beginning to gather a sense of self. Was that because she was recalling things on a subliminal level or was it because she'd just gotten used to living in a world less than a week old?

Was that why Simon seemed like a friend?

Was that what he seemed, or was it something a whole lot more and growing exponentially every moment?

"We're getting off here," he said suddenly, and she realized she'd been in a state so close to sleep his voice startled her. A glance out the window showed morning had come while she languished in a stupor. The narrow streets of the waterside town through which they traveled appeared all but abandoned.

"This isn't Seattle, is it?"

"No, but it's 6:00 a.m. and we just passed a car rental place. Let's go."

They walked the three blocks back to the rental agency, which was just opening for business. "Give me half an hour," the proprietor pleaded. "I gotta get things straightened away. We don't usually open until seven."

Simon looked down at her. "Are you hungry?"

"Sure," she said.

"There's a little diner right around the corner," the rental man offered.

At the door to the diner, Simon put some coins into a newspaper machine and extracted the *Portland Oregonian* newspaper. He scanned the front page, then tucked it beneath his arm and held the door for her.

The moment the warm, food-laden air hit her nose, Ella's stomach rolled over like a lazy giant getting out of bed. A giant in a foul mood.

"You okay?" Simon asked as they sat across from each other at a table near the back.

"I thought it was the medicine I take at night that made me nauseated in the morning," she said, "but I guess not. I didn't take it last night, so it can't be that."

"Maybe it's your head injury," he said quickly.

"And this nausea just comes around in the morning?"

"I don't know," he said, "except that this hasn't exactly been a normal morning, has it?"

"How do I know? Maybe I run away from thugs and husbands every day of my life."

A smile tugged his lips. "Do you want to leave?"

"I'm afraid so."

"I'll get a coffee to go."

"I'll visit the restroom and see if I can peel off a bandage or two. If my face is the key to people telling me what's going on with my father, I'd better try to make more of it visible."

As soon as Ella disappeared into the ladies' room, Simon opened the *Oregonian*. The front page offered nothing enlightening. He quickly scanned the A section, pausing only to order a large coffee to go.

The story was buried on page seven. The victim's name was Jerry Bucker, found murdered days earlier in a field Simon knew to be less than a half mile from Ella's house.

Jerry Bucker. Hadn't the old man in the restaurant said the contact Ella met before she lost her memory was a guy named Jerry? And hadn't he said no one had seen or heard from Jerry since that contact?

This revelation seemed to nail Ella against the wall.

His phone vibrated in his pocket. It was Devin on the other end and he led off with a question. "Did you hear the police want Ella as a person of interest in the death of a man dumped near her house the day you think she disappeared?"

Simon ran a hand over his face as though he could wipe away all the confusion and doubt. "Yeah, I heard. There's not much in the paper."

"It was big news a few days ago. I don't know why I didn't think to connect the murder to her right from the start, but the cops are bound to find out I've been asking questions."

"Tell them as little as you can without endangering your license," Simon said.

"It might help if you hired me."

"You're hired. First thing I'd appreciate you doing is contacting the Cozy Comfort Motel in Witchit and making arrangements for my truck to be stored there and not towed away."

"Sure."

"What do you know about the victim?"

"Probably not much more than you know. Former cop from Chicago, late sixties, retired up along the Columbia River. No one seems to know why he was in Blue Mountain."

"How was he killed?"

"The police aren't saying. I don't know why they're so closemouthed on this. You could probably call your partner—"

"No. I won't get Mike into this. Do you know what connected Jerry Bucker to Ella?"

"They're not saying, but word on the street was his car was seen in front of her house and since she's gone, it looks suspicious."

"That's a very loose connection."

"Your girl still batting zero with the memory?"

"More or less. No way she can explain what a dead man was doing visiting her when she can't remember who she is."

"There's something else. Probably unrelated,

but after missing the connection last time, I'm not taking any chances."

"What are you talking about?"

"There was an old guy found dead in his car at a parking lot in Rocky Point a few days ago. Isn't that where you said you were? Anyway, his last name was Connors, first name Robert. Ring any bells?"

"Where was the car?"

"North of town, out by a restaurant. Seemed emergency vehicles responded to a call about a woman going off the bluff and a guy going to her rescue. By the time they got there, the woman and her rescuer were gone. That's when someone noticed the old man in the car with a slit throat."

"Oh, God."

"I don't like the sound of that," Devin said.

"If it's the man I think it is, I know who killed him."

"Who?"

"I don't know a name, I just know a face."

"You have got to start thinking about yourself," Devin warned.

"Ditto. I'm going to get to the bottom of this in four or five hours and then I'll figure out the best way to go to the authorities. Don't call me anymore, I'll call you on a pay phone. From now on, the cell is out."

"Yeah, okay. I kept coming up against a wall

while looking into Ella's background," Devin said as the waitress delivered Simon's coffee and took his money. "It looks to me like she went to some trouble to distance herself from her past. I don't even think we got her maiden name right. Now that I know Jerry Bucker was a former cop in Chicago, I can do some digging back there and see what I come up with."

Handing over his debit card, Simon said, "Just be careful."

He snapped the phone shut and this time turned off the power. He was grabbing a couple of napkins when he saw Ella emerge from the ladies' room. She'd removed a couple of the bandages and combed her hair, and despite the fatigue and scratches, she positively glowed as the morning sun filtered through the window and bathed the delicate bone structure of her face.

God, how he'd once loved her. He'd looked past the things that drove him crazy and basked in the simple joy of being with her. The qualms he should have acknowledged right from the beginning he'd buried under blithe rationale. She would come around. She would open up. She would love him for who he was….

A knot formed in his throat as she approached.

She was depending on him to help her find the one person in the world she remembered.

Had Carl killed Jerry Bucker and forced Ella to come with him? Was that why she'd left the clues at her place, the lights on, the snow globe in the empty garage? Or were those inconsequential oversights in her rush to leave her house? Was she in this deeper than he could imagine? There were two murders now, two dead men, both of whom saw Ella right before their deaths. But at least he knew she couldn't have killed the second contact.

Did he? She'd disappeared outside for five minutes before Carl gave up paying the bill and went to find her….

No. This was impossible. That would mean she was faking the amnesia and he knew she wasn't; he'd bet his life on it.

His career…

"You look very worried," Ella said as she paused in front of him.

Resisting the urge to cup her face, to plead with her to remember something, anything, he reached for the door and held it open for her. "Just anxious," he said as they hurried back to the rental place.

THEY MADE IT TO TAMPOO with enough time to stop at a shopping mall. Ella loved the violet-blue tunic she found and wore it out of the store with her new jeans and a pair of sturdy walking shoes. She couldn't help but wonder if she always had such a hard time finding pants that fit in the waist.

They stopped at a men's store next. While Simon disappeared into the back, Ella looked through a rack of shirts. She found a dark gray one that would match Simon's eyes, just as her new tunic matched hers. When she looked around the store for him, she discovered he was already at the counter making a purchase.

Once outside, he stopped at a secluded bench, took a red-and-navy plaid flannel shirt from the bag and started pulling off tags.

"That's what you chose?" she asked, smiling. "Instead of the pretty gray shirt I found, you bought something my father would wear to chop wood?"

"Is that a specific memory or a generalization?" he asked.

She sagged onto the bench. "I remember my dad wearing a shirt like that one. I must have been ten or eleven and we were going to go cut a Christmas tree at a farm. There was a boy there, too, older than me, with dark hair, but he kind of ran ahead."

"I wonder if the boy is your brother."

"Maybe. I just remember staying with my father, holding his hand. I can hear a woman's voice say, 'Such a daddy's girl.' Being with my dad was all that mattered." She wiped a couple of warm tears from her eyes as the memory seemed to wrap its arms around her.

"You're getting older in each memory," Simon said softly.

"I noticed that. The way they just pop into my head as unrelated pieces of flotsam and then sucker punch me with the emotion that follows is unnerving. Wow, I really adore my dad. He must be a huge part of my life."

Buttoning the shirt over the T-shirt he'd started the day in, Simon grabbed a burgundy cap from the bag, as well. With the big flannel shirt and the cap pulled over his dark hair, he looked different.

"You bought yourself a disguise," she said. "The dark stubble on your jaw is a good touch."

"You think so?"

She looked down at her hands, suddenly swamped with a feeling of fear and despair. He sat down beside her. "What is it, Ella?"

"Why is my father going about reaching me in such a dangerous way? The guy back in Rocky Point said my father needed me. And what about my mother? Where is she?"

"Do you remember her?"

Ella clasped a hand to her chest as she nodded, more surprised by the realization she did remember her mother than by the significance of the actual memory. "It was her calling me a daddy's girl," she said, her voice hushed. "She had deep blue eyes and faint freckles. How can I remember nothing about her but her face and voice and so much about my father but not what he looked like?"

"It's curious, isn't it?"

She reached over and took Simon's hand, turning his wrist so she could see his watch, but enjoying the contact with his warm skin too much to let go. "We only have an hour before we meet the next contact. What about Carl and the other man? What could they possibly want with my dad?"

He shook his head as his fingers closed around hers. The motion sent heat waves up her arm and she looked at his face, at his mouth, and heaven help her, but she wished she could kiss him.

"I don't have answers for you," he said softly.

"Do you think the contact will be in danger?"

His look at her was sharp. "Why do you ask that?"

"Because the one back at the restaurant said no one had heard from the first man who came to see me. His name was Jerry."

Her stomach fluttered as something shifted in Simon's eyes. "What aren't you telling me?" She withdrew her hand and tucked it into a pocket.

"Nothing."

"You're lying."

"Okay," he said with a sigh, "I'm lying." He

started stuffing tags and papers into the sack as he slid her a sidelong glance. "Listen, Ella, you've trusted me so far, trust me a little while longer."

"I'm trying," she said.

"I know." He looked in her eyes. His were the color of granite today. He added, "You don't have to go to this meeting. We can get the police involved. They can meet your father's contact and capture Carl and the big guy. You don't have to do it."

"But my father—"

"Is not worth risking your life or safety."

"We've been through this. If you'll give me a ride to the depot, I'll take it from there. You can go on your way."

He cast her an impatient look. "Okay, we'll do it your way on one condition. I want to case the place before you enter. I'm sure Carl and what's his name will be there, but I think they'll think twice about trying anything in public."

"And Carl knows I have to speak to the contact alone, don't forget that."

"Right. They'll make their move afterward, out in the open. That's when they'll try to grab you."

"Have you figured out why Carl wanted to jump the gun last night?"

"My best guess is he wanted to control the situation going in."

"What does that mean, you know, in real person talk?"

"It means he's going to have to try to nab you today in broad daylight in a public place. If he'd gotten you last night, he might have been able to arrange the situation at the depot to his liking."

Her eyes grew wide. "I wonder if he's been giving me some kind of sedative or something, you know, to make me more submissive. Maybe that's why my stomach hurts half the day."

Simon's dark eyes flashed, and for a second, dressed as he was, his handsome face rough with beard, he looked more dangerous than comforting. "The bastard better hope like hell he didn't," he said, standing abruptly as though a powder keg in his body suddenly exploded. He grabbed her hand. "Come on, babe, it's time to go. Let's get this over with."

The unexpected and casual endearment caught her off guard, but the surprise was short-lived, followed by a warm feeling of certainty.

She'd asked herself a question the night before, a question she hadn't been able to answer, but now she could.

Yes. Somewhere, someone either loved her now or had loved her in the past.

And that someone wasn't Carl Baxter.

Chapter Eight

The Tampoo Bus Station occupied half a block of Second and Pearl in downtown Tampoo with large garages running at right angles to each other, surrounding what appeared from the outside to be the main lobby. An abandoned café took corner space with its own street entrance, boarded up now, windows blacked out.

There were three large buses occupying the garage area, including one with its engine compartment open. A truck with the logo Mobile Bus Mechanics was backed up to the bus. Three men in coveralls carried lunch boxes toward a cluster of trees in the far corner of the parking lot.

Simon had finally convinced Ella to lie down on the backseat so it would appear he was alone in the car in case Carl Baxter or the big guy with the knife happened to be watching and recognized him. The plaid shirt and hat weren't a very sophisticated disguise. He just hoped Ella was right about the dark stubble blurring the contours of his face. He drove slowly past the depot, pulling to the curb half a block farther on.

Turning in the seat, he peered into the back. Ella's huge blue eyes looked stark against her pale complexion. "Give me five minutes," he said, slipping his wallet into the glove box. He'd decided not to carry identification, though he wasn't clear why he'd made that decision. Was he still trying to protect his job? That seemed idiotic, but he locked his wallet in the glove box anyway and turned to hand Ella his watch.

She pulled it over her hand. "I'll just lie here and listen to my heart pound in my ears."

"Try not to look for me when you enter the depot. Judging from the original two contacts, this one will be another older man…."

The words were out of his mouth when he realized what he'd just done, that he'd told her he knew what her original contact, Jerry Bucker, now dead, had looked like.

"How do you know how old Jerry was?" she asked.

"I just know."

"Because you saw him at my house? Oh, God, Simon, were you there?"

"No, I wasn't there, I promise."

"Simon—"

And suddenly, Simon knew he couldn't send her into the bus depot and harm's way without being honest with her. She had a right to know what she was getting into. Maybe she'd change her mind if she realized how dangerous it was. "Because an older guy named Jerry Bucker is dead," he said simply. "It was in the morning paper."

Did he mention Robert Connors's stabbing death in Rocky Point? He wasn't positive it was the same man who had met with Ella though the law of coincidence leaned heavily in that direction. One glance at her face made the decision—that news could wait.

She closed her eyes and her words were blurred as she muttered, "When did he die? Where?"

"Days ago, back in Blue Mountain. His body was found in a vacant lot."

Her eyes fluttered open. "I think I saw it on television. Carl turned the TV off, but I think I saw the recovery of the man's body. Who killed him?"

"They don't know."

"How was he killed?"

"They're not saying."

"Oh, my God. Did I have something to do with his death? I can't remember—"

"I'm sure you didn't," Simon said.

"How can you be sure?"

How *could* he be sure? Truth: he couldn't. He said, "I just know it in my heart," and hoped she believed him. Before she could go further with this, he added, "Listen, it's getting late. Do you want to go through with this or do you want to drive away?"

"I can't drive away," she said, determination stealing back into her voice. "I have to find my father."

"Then give me five minutes," he said, "and when you meet this contact, warn him, okay?"

"Yes, of course."

Simon locked the doors as he exited the car. The first order of business was to walk around the building making notes of exits. He passed a room with lockers visible inside and several doors with chains and padlocks and no clue as to where they led. Once he had a feeling for the exterior, he entered the building.

The interior door to the abandoned café was right inside, occupying a front corner. Through the glass insert in the wood doors, Simon could make out stacks of dusty chairs. The doors were chained and locked.

The ticket counter, with a few people lined up in front of it, was to his left. He parked himself behind a young couple holding hands and proceeded to pat his pockets as though looking for his wallet or a misplaced ticket. While doing that, he surreptitiously looked around the place.

Five iron benches took up the center of the waiting area while a few plastic chairs and a couple of vending machines and arcade games were scattered against the walls. Five or six people sat in various states of boredom.

A minute later, the restroom door opened, disgorging a tall man with brownish skin wearing a tan raincoat. It took Simon a second to recognize him, and as soon as he did, he turned his face against the wall. It was the man with the knife. He'd shaven off his beard and looked younger, his face thinner, but Simon would know those intense black eyes anywhere. The man immediately made his way to a vending machine, where another peek revealed him making a show of studying snack choices. Simon saw how often his gaze went to the doors. There was no sign of Carl.

Okay, he hadn't expected them to come inside the depot. As far as he knew, Carl and the guy with the knife were just as anxious for Ella to get her next message as Ella was. He'd thought for sure they'd wait until she stepped outside. He guessed the man with the knife was there just to make sure Ella was covered when the meeting was over.

Simon scanned the gathering for a sign of an elderly man who might be the contact. Everyone was too young with the exception of one person, but that person was female and sat with her back against a wall with her eyes closed.

Simon moved up a step in line just as the door opened and Ella walked inside. Their formerly bearded adversary visibly stiffened at the sight of her and he looked away quickly. Ella chose a deserted bench in the middle of the room and sat down. She didn't look at anyone else, keeping her gaze directed at Simon's watch. She'd pushed it up her arm, where it was held in place by the bunched sleeve of her thick knit shirt. He could practically see her trembling.

The wall clock seemed to click the minutes off at glacial speed. Noon came and went. A bus emptied several people into the waiting area. Others left to get on a departing bus. An older man wearing a feather in his cap entered from the street and looked around carefully, and for a moment, Simon thought they had their contact, but a teenager by one of the arcade games yelled, "Grandpa!" The two hugged and left together.

If Jerry Bucker's death was well known, perhaps the contact had decided this was all too dangerous. A profound moment of relief quickly went up in smoke as an old guy with a newspaper rolled in one hand entered the depot through the same door Ella had used.

Simon knew the older man was ex-police by the

way he carried himself. He might be retired but he was still wary, a man used to assessing everything and everyone around him. Simon would bet his life on the fact that the man was armed and ready to defend himself.

But he didn't expect what happened next. The old guy's gaze lingered on the bulky shape of the man with the knife so long, the other man sensed it and looked over his shoulder. Their gazes met and flashed away, but surprised recognition singed the air between them. The old guy immediately looked toward the door as though trying to decide what to do while the big man turned his back.

What was going on? They knew each other?

The older man apparently reached a decision. Walking quickly now, he approached Ella, sat down and started speaking. As she nodded and leaned closer to him, the man shook open his newspaper and the two of them disappeared behind it.

Once again Simon located the man he'd first seen on the bluff wielding a knife only a little over twenty-four hours before. He'd moved to a different vending machine and was dropping in coins, but by the way his gaze was glued to the glass panel of the machine, Simon was pretty sure he was really watching the reflection of the meeting going on across the room. There was still no sign of Carl, who was probably waiting outside to spring a trap once Ella left.

Simon had long since stepped out of the line and found an obscure corner. As he waited for the meeting to be over, he counted how many people were now in the depot. Including the woman selling tickets behind the counter, there were ten. At least four of them were here because of this meeting. That left six possibly unrelated individuals.

The newspaper moved as the old man rolled it once again and placed it on the seat next to him. Ella looked strained but resolved. The ex-cop patted her arm before getting to his feet. As he stood, his gaze darted to the big guy, who turned and took a step toward him.

The older woman who had seemed to be asleep also stood and joined the man, linking her arm with his. The big guy stopped abruptly. The older couple moved in unison toward the door. Apparently, news of Jerry Bucker's and maybe Robert Connors's deaths had reached Tampoo.

If so, what kind of loyalty propelled these old guys to risk themselves this way? And why were they being murdered *after* they spoke to Ella?

The big guy formed a fist and knocked it against his thigh. With hatred burning in his eyes, he turned his attention to Ella.

But Ella was looking at Simon, and though he tried to telegraph a warning, she looked away too quickly. He'd have to manually stop her from proceeding out the front doors, because that path would take her too close to the man in the raincoat, who appeared angry enough to throttle someone.

Simon heard passengers disembarking in the garage area behind him. Any second, they would barge through the doors. If he could waylay Ella, the two of them could get lost in the small crowd outside and circle the block back to their car. All he had to do was intercept her….

The metal door connecting garage and waiting area swung open. Several people flooded through, including a frail but spry white-haired woman using a four-wheeled walker who stopped right in front of Simon.

"What's the time?" she demanded.

He glanced at the clock. "Twelve-forty," he said, trying to get past the walker without bumping the woman.

"Where's my son? He's late. He's always late."

Over her head, Simon saw the tall man paralleling Ella's path. She appeared to be totally unaware of his presence.

"Excuse me," he added, sidling past the walker as he slid his hand under his jacket, unhooking the strap that held his revolver in the holster. There was no way he would pull a gun in a crowded building, but he suspected the big guy would usher Ella outside into Carl's waiting arms.

He'd see about that.

Instead, the man suddenly sped up and purposely rammed into Ella. She stumbled and turned to look up at him. Simon heard her intake of breath as the man placed huge hands on her arms. She seemed to sag against him.

Simon yelled, "Hey!" but it was drowned in the bellowing tones of the giant.

"Honey?" the big man said as he scooped Ella up like a rag doll. "Are you okay? You need fresh air." He knocked the door open with his broad back, supporting Ella's weight, his gaze briefly meeting Simon's. Simon looked at Ella's face. Her eyes were open, his lips moved, but the big man's continuing assurances covered whatever she was trying to say.

Simon had seen the man slip something into his pocket. He'd drugged her. He'd stuck the needle or whatever delivery system he'd chosen back in his pocket and covered her collapse with his booming voice and tan raincoat. That had to be what happened.

Simon quickened his pace. Damn. He'd screwed up; he hadn't expected they would make their move inside the building. A young boy ran into the station as Ella disappeared outside. The kid bumped against Simon's legs. Simon caught him and turned him away from the doors. "Slow down, buddy," he said.

The kid opened his mouth to speak, but the words never came. At that instant, an explosion rocked the building, blowing out the café doors. Simon, snatched from his feet, was hurtled against the ticket counter. Screams were followed by falling debris and frantic calls for help. The boy lay on the floor nearby. Simon crawled to him, clearing dust off his face and urging him to take slow, steady breaths. He couldn't see that any of the glass had hit the kid, who seemed more dazed than hurt.

A woman appeared through the gaping hole in the depot wall. "Peter!" she screamed, frantically looking every direction.

"Over here," Simon said hopefully.

She was there in a flash. "Peter, you ran ahead of me—oh, Peter!" She fell to her knees, taking the boy into her arms.

"Keep him still until help arrives," Simon urged.

She cast him an alarmed glance. "What happened?"

"A bomb, I think." He struggled to his feet, relieved to see the boy trying to sit up.

The woman caught Simon's wrist. "You're

hurt," she said. "The back of your shirt is bloody. You'd better stay still."

"Can't," he said, peering through the gaping hole in the wall in time to see the tail end of a man shoving Ella's limp body into the backseat of a car.

"No," Simon yelled, but it was more of a croak. Behind him, pandemonium reigned; people sobbed and shrieked. As the car carrying Ella eased back into traffic, Simon staggered down the sidewalk toward his own vehicle, his head echoing with the concussion of the explosion, his movements unsteady and way too slow.

He heard approaching sirens. Pedestrians pushed past him on their way toward the depot. Fire and smoke filled the air. Traffic began plugging the street, but Simon could see the car Ella had been pushed into and it was still moving, ahead of most of the congestion.

A Harley pulled up alongside the curb in front of Simon. Throwing his feet to the ground and turning to look back, the driver tore off his helmet, revealing a head full of long dark hair. He was about Simon's age and very tan. He said, "Get on."

Simon wiped his face, barely noticing when his hand came away covered in blood. "What?"

"Get on," the man repeated with a slight accent.

"Who—"

"Your car is blocked in. If you want to save

Ella, get on the bike. *Ahora.*" He pulled his helmet back on his head and revved the engine. Simon covered the remaining sidewalk as fast as his shocked and battered body could take him. He climbed on behind the stranger, who pulled back onto the street a second later, weaving the big bike through the stalled cars, moving quickly toward the corner.

ELLA SAGGED AGAINST THE MAN sitting next to her. Her brain was scrambled like morning eggs, but she did know a couple of things. She knew she wasn't supposed to be in this car and she knew the man holding her down on the seat was the same man who had bumped into her at the bus depot.

Another man turned around from the driver's seat and grinned at her. She recalled him at once, though it was hard to place him. Long blond hair gathered into a ponytail, long nose, thin lips. He looked at her for a heartbeat, then turned back to driving. Over his shoulder he said, "Did you give her the drug I bought on the street?"

"Half of it. She's not very big."

The driver grumbled. "It appears to be working. Slap her, don't let her fall asleep. Not yet."

A hand appeared out of nowhere. The slap came quick and strong, snapping her head back against the seat, bringing water to her eyes, but it couldn't dispel the bone-chilling lethargy that frosted her veins like an advancing glacier.

"Did she meet with an old man?" the voice from the front demanded.

"Yeah, and get this, it was Potter."

"I don't know anyone named Potter."

The big man grunted. "I keep forgetting you're in this for the money and nothing else."

"No shame in that," the driver said. Ella stared at the back of his head. A ponytail. She knew him. Carl. His name was Carl.

"The bastard got away," the big man grumbled.

"He's not important," the detached voice said.

He was her husband.

"He is to me. They all are. But I'll find him, you wait and see."

There was a pause as Ella touched her face, almost surprised when her fingers found skin instead of bones. What was wrong with her? Why couldn't she think?

"Where are you meeting the next contact, Eleanor?" the man in the front asked.

"Idaho," she mumbled, vaguely alarmed she'd responded and terribly sleepy.

"Where in Idaho?"

"Storm Creek." Her voice seemed to come from somewhere outside her body, like maybe from an overhead speaker.

The front-seat man snapped, "When?"

Before she could answer, her seat companion leaned forward. "The freeway ramp is up ahead."

"I see it. When, Eleanor?"

"Tomorrow," she whispered. She had a deep-down feeling she should refuse to answer any questions posed by these men, but she was unable to stop herself. All she really wanted was to lie down....

With a hard turn, the car, which had been veering right, suddenly swerved the other direction and she slid against the opposite door. A loud roar outside the window evolved into a motorcycle right beside the car. Carl swore as he steered the car under a bridge, missing the ramp completely.

"Damn it! He cut us off!"

There was a lot more swearing. Both men sounded furious. "What time is the meeting?" Carl demanded. "Eleanor, what time?"

She tried to close her eyes and ignore the raised voices and the demands, but the big man beside her grabbed her shoulders and shook her.

"Three o'clock," she muttered.

"What? What did she say?"

"Three," the big man yelled as he twisted to look out the rear window. "That bike is still back there."

"I know. And there's roadwork ahead. Look for someplace we can turn around."

"Up ahead, to the left, some old plant of some kind."

"Yeah, I see it. Hold on."

The car soon made another hard turn, the tires squealing. A loud metallic sound was followed by pieces of chain flying past the windows as the car broke through the rusted barrier and bounced on the uneven pavement of what had once been a parking lot.

"You got a gun?" the driver yelled.

"Just the knife. Gun in the trunk."

More squealing tires, more yelling, the big man twisting again, hands bunched, knots in his massive jaw. "They're still back there."

"I know, I know. Get her head down, protect her face."

The car skidded as it turned again. The big man pushed Ella's head toward the seat. She felt an odd sense of detachment, a floating sensation as though only her body were in the car.

And yet at the same time a tiny fire flickered in her gut, a defiant flame braving the storm, beginning to spread warmth through her body again. In her mind, she walked toward the flame.

The dark figure of a man stood beside the rippling light, hand extended. She couldn't see his face, but his voice bathed her with comfort. He leaned down and said, *It's all right. Every-*

thing is better. I'm sorry, sweetheart. I won't leave again.

Daddy?

The answer to her hushed question came in the form of a hand clamping down on her wrist, propelling her mind back to the inside of the car. The big man opened the door and jumped out, pulling Ella along after him. A scream died in her throat as she realized the vehicle was no longer moving. Her legs folded beneath her.

The big man bundled her against him like an armload of sticks and carried her around to the back of the car, where Carl was hiding. He held a big gun.

The next thing she knew, thunder roared from above as a huge black shape flew over her head and crashed somewhere in the distance. She covered her ears with her hands, melting into the gritty pavement, finally free to close her eyes where once again the flickering flame drew her to its warmth and the promise of her father's voice.

Chapter Nine

Simon knew Carl was at the wheel; he'd seen the man when the bike prevented the car from taking the on-ramp. He hadn't been able to see in the backseat, but he knew Ella was back there.

Where would they take her? How could they go too far without finding out what she knew about the next meeting place?

His cell phone practically burned in his pocket. Things had gone too far. He'd let them go too far. Better Ella should be safe in a jail than in this situation. She couldn't have murdered Jerry Bucker, she couldn't be in cahoots with Carl Baxter…

But she could.

Carl wouldn't give her anything that would disable her too long until they knew what she'd learned from the contact and which direction to travel next. That meant just enough to control her for a while and hopefully, hopefully, that meant it wouldn't hurt her baby….

The road grew increasingly industrial and un-traveled. Orange signs announced roadwork ahead, and even over the noise of the Harley engine, Simon could make out the sound of earth-moving equipment. The car was going to have to turn around or risk being delayed, and Simon doubted very much they would take such a chance.

Up ahead of them, the car made a tight right turn into a vast parking lot, kicking up gravel and a dirt cloud as it bounced over torn patches of old asphalt, headed for the river where the hulking shape of a long sheet metal building abutted an aging wharf. Rotting piers jutted out of the gray waters of Puget Sound. It appeared to be an old fish packing plant.

The car went in a straight line toward the wharf. With the motorcycle, however, caution had to be used lest the bike spin out of control on buckled pavement and patches of loose gravel. Up ahead, Simon saw the car come to a screeching halt in front of the largest structure. Two men jumped out of the vehicle, the larger shape manhandling Ella to the protection of the far side. Simon saw the flash of a gun in Carl's hand. Shots whizzed past the cycle.

The Harley driver veered to the left, running the bike up a ramp that ran behind Carl and his buddy, bursting into the gutted shell of the structure behind them.

Simon was off the bike before it had completely stopped, stumbling once and catching himself on an overturned barrel. Revolver in hand, he knew he had to disable the car immediately. He darted to a glassless window and chanced a peek, but from this angle all he could see was the hood of the car.

The biker came up behind him, helmet removed. "What's the plan?" he asked, his voice deep and flavored slightly with a Spanish accent.

"Shoot a couple of tires out of the car, subdue the two men, rescue Ella."

"I'm not armed." He rubbed his jaw and added, "Be prepared, amigo." In the next instant, he'd sprung to his feet and disappeared into the deep shadows of the building, his footsteps all but inaudible, which was amazing considering the condition of the floor.

Simon didn't waste time shaking his head, but that's what he felt like doing. Be prepared? What, like a Boy Scout? Didn't look as though there was going to be a lot of help from that quarter after all. He shot a few rounds through the window opening just to announce his intentions, inserted a new clip and made for the door. If that car left again with Ella inside it, who knew what would happen? He had to disable the car.

From the door of the building, he moved to the shelter of a row of old steel drums. From there he could see the right side of the car. A bullet ricocheted off one drum. He shot out the rear tire, then aimed for the front.

Before he could pull the trigger, a man's voice announced, "One more shot and Eleanor dies."

Simon's trigger finger froze in place. He heard sounds of a struggle and then Carl appeared down below, in back of the car, a drooping Ella held in front of him as a shield. Her eyes fluttered open. Carl looped one of his arms around her neck while he pressed a gun barrel against her temple. Her expression immediately jumped from dazed to terrified.

"You won't kill her," Simon yelled. "You want to know what she knows. You need her face to open doors."

"You're right," Carl yelled, "I can't kill her. But I can wound her. What do you think? Leg? An arm?" Ella's gasps as Carl jabbed the muzzle harder into the side of her head skittered along Simon's nerve endings like firecrackers.

"Or maybe Chopper could use his knife on her, you know, someplace it won't show," Carl added.

Even from that distance, Simon could see the skin around Ella's lips grow white.

"Make up your mind!" Carl yelled, clasping her even closer to his body. "Drop your gun and stand up."

Decision time again.

Who was he trying to kid? Making a decision implied options, and he had none, but still, the first rule of police work was never to surrender a weapon.

"You win, Baxter," he shouted, bending slowly, putting the gun down carefully, sliding it into view. As he straightened up, he kept his eyes on Ella. Every bone in her face seemed to push against her ashen skin.

"Now you're being reasonable," Carl said, a smug smile playing over his lips. Raising his voice, he added, "Chopper, where are you?"

The big man who had abducted Ella from the bus depot sauntered out of the building behind Simon. The only thing more imposing than the size of Chopper was the curved cold steel knife he held in one hand.

"Where's the other guy?" Carl demanded.

"I found him hiding out by the old pier," Chopper yelled.

"Did you get rid of him?"

"I'm not a killer," the big man yelled. As his knife was one millimeter from severing Simon's future, Simon was happy to hear it.

Then he remembered Robert Connors found stabbed to death in his car.

"Since when?" Carl quipped as though the same thought had occurred to him.

"That's different and you know it. I'm not the one who set off a bomb at the depot."

"We all serve our own gods, Chopper. So, the bottom line is you left someone free to do what he wants."

Chopper pulled a roll of gray duct tape from his pocket. "No, I took care of him. He isn't going anywhere."

Simon hadn't held out a lot of hope for his Spanish-speaking friend with the light eyes, but now it looked as though there was no hope at all. He swallowed hard as Chopper grabbed him by the upper arm and marched him down the ramp. The tip of the knife blade was so close to his spine he could feel it all the way to his belly button and found himself arching his back as he walked.

Ella's eyes widened as she got a good look at him. "Are you all right?" she asked, her voice slurred.

"Couldn't be better. How about you?"

She managed a fleeting smile.

Carl yanked her closer again, strangling her for a second. "Chopper, check his wallet."

"He doesn't have one," Chopper grumbled after none too gently patting Simon down. The slaps jarred Simon's mincemeat back, causing shivers to shoot through his body. He was suddenly very glad he'd decided to leave his wallet in the car.

"So, just who in the devil are you?" Carl asked as Chopper once again loomed right behind Simon.

"A friend."

"Well, friend, you just bought yourself a load of trouble. If you'd left my wife at the motel last night, we could have wired her before she met the old guy today and none of this would have been necessary."

"Would that be before or after she fell to her death off the bluff?" Simon asked.

Carl shook his head. "It doesn't matter who you are. It's obvious you've turned into Eleanor's knight in shining armor. You're going to wish you'd kept your nose in your own business."

"You don't need to hurt her," Simon said, his fists clenched so hard his blunt nails bit into his palms. "She's not going anywhere, you know that. Loosen your grip. She's just as innocent—"

A bark of laughter escaped Carl. "My wife innocent. How quaint."

"I can't be your wife," Ella said, eyes gaining a little bit of the old flash. "I wouldn't marry someone like you."

"I have the papers to prove it, sweetheart."

"You left me on a cliff to die and now you have a gun pointed at my head. Some marriage."

He smiled again. Putting his lips close to Ella's ear, he added, "You've already told me everything

I need to know about the next contact except where the meeting is to take place. Tell me that or I shoot your new friend."

"You'll kill me anyway," Simon said, still gazing at Ella.

Carl's voice dipped to a smooth, intimate tone, as he leaned in closer still. "Your friend is right, I probably will kill him anyway. But there are all sorts of ways to die, some a lot slower and more painful than others. How about it? Have you ever seen a kneecap explode?"

She shook her head.

"And whatever I do to him, I'll do to your father when I find him. With or without your help, I will find him. You can make it easier on me and you can make it easier on your father. Your choice."

"What do you want my father for? What did he do to you?"

"To me? Nothing. I just want to talk with him, that's all."

"Before or after you blow up his kneecap?"

Simon smiled internally. The old Ella was making a comeback.

"Maybe a little of the hero's blood will loosen her tongue," Carl said, leveling his gaze at Simon. "Go ahead, Chopper, use your knife."

Chopper raised the knife to Simon's throat, but he paused. "You want him dead, you kill him." He lowered the blade and pushed Simon ahead of him. The pressure of his hand hitting Simon's back felt like a million razor blades slicing through his skin.

They came to a stop a few feet short of Carl and Ella. "I'm in this for one reason, and you know it," Chopper growled. "I agreed to join up with you just to expedite my cause. That means I take care of the men who wronged me. They're mine. Someone like this man? He's yours."

"Why?" Simon asked. "And what is it you two want so much? I mean, besides spreading misery and mayhem, what is it you're both after?"

He was totally ignored as the two men glared at each other. Hoping to capitalize on their mutual animosity, he added, "You guys weren't buddies on the cliff. You were trying to kill each other. That's got to make trusting each other kind of tricky."

Carl cast him a withering look. Well, okay, it had been an amateurish attempt to play them against each other, but what other choice did he have? How could he possibly disarm both men? Carl might have relaxed his hold on Ella a little, but the gun was still positioned at her temple.

Carl finally spoke. "We're a team," he told Chopper. "I'll prove it. I'll kill the Good Samaritan." The clicking sound as he cocked the gun seemed to shoot through Simon.

"Wait! Okay, okay, I'll tell you," Ella gasped. "The meeting is at the last restaurant leaving Storm Creek going north."

"What's its name?"

"The Red Barron. No, the Red Barn. That's what it is, the Red Barn. Don't hurt him."

Carl rocked back on his feet, grinning. "That's my girl." Addressing Chopper, he added, "The leftovers from the bomb-making material and the receipts for all the equipment are in the trunk. Get them. We'll set the Samaritan up inside that building with all the evidence and stage a little suicide. That ought to take care of a couple of loose ends at once."

"But you said—" Ella began.

Carl kissed the back of her neck. "Since when did you get so gullible, sweetheart?" Once again addressing Chopper, he added, "Use that tape you have to gag and bind my wife first. We'll leave her in the car."

As Chopper once again began ranting about Baxter's tendency to issue orders, Simon glanced at Ella. There was a cold, detached look creeping into her eyes. If Simon was a betting man, he'd lay odds she was a breath away from trying to break free from Carl. It might work. The man was so disdainful of her strength of will, he might underestimate her, and from his position, he couldn't see the anger brewing in her face. He shouldn't have made fun of her, shouldn't have kissed her neck…

Simon had no idea how far she would get, but that wasn't the point. He was pretty sure Carl wouldn't risk shooting her.

Did she realize no one had picked his gun up from where he'd slid it? He didn't dare turn around and look, but he knew it was there. Chopper hadn't bent over to retrieve it. If she could make it to the ramp and remember the gun, she'd be armed.

A roaring noise seemed to come from nowhere. Simon looked up in time to see the motorcycle burst out of the dilapidated building behind the car and fly over them, missing Carl's head by less than a foot. The helmeted rider landed the bike with a jolt. Skidding, he turned the big machine and headed back, aimed at Carl.

As Simon looked around for Ella, he saw her fling her head back hard, hitting Carl in the nose. Between the advancing bike and the sudden impact on his face, Carl's grip loosened enough for Ella to break free. The two thugs dived for cover as Simon grabbed Ella's good hand and dragged her up the ramp, retrieving his revolver on the way. His aching body was forgotten in the need to find something better to hide behind than rusty metal and rotting wood.

Outside, he heard shouting and the sound of an engine. They had almost reached the far end of the building when the motorcycle appeared in the sunlit opening on the end they were nearest to, the sound deafening as it tore up to within a few feet of them.

Ella tensed as she stepped back against Simon. She was heaving. He knew exactly how she felt.

Without turning off the engine, the rider tore off the helmet and looked at each of them, his gaze lingering on Ella.

"Who *are* you?" Simon demanded.

"The name is Jack."

"Do I know you?" Ella said.

"No, *cariño,*" he answered after a brief pause. He handed the helmet to Ella and added, "Put this on." Pieces of gray tape hung from his wrists and circled the hem of his jeans.

"Get her out of here now," Simon said.

"I'm not going, you are," Jack said as he slid off the big bike. He touched Ella's arm and motioned her to climb aboard.

She paused. "But what about you?"

"I'm staying here." He looked at Simon and added, "The very large man found himself an automatic, I guess in the car, so now they're both armed."

"I can't leave you—"

"No time to argue," Jack said.

"Then take my gun."

Jack threw up his hands. "No, no gun. I don't need that kind of grief."

Simon stuck the weapon in his belt. "I'll call the police as soon as I get away from here," he said.

"No police." The response was quick and adamant.

What was it with everybody suddenly hating cops? "Listen," Simon said, "those men are murderers. Then there's the bomb—"

"No police," Jack repeated. "You heard Baxter, you heard him say Ella was involved in this. Until you find out how deeply, no cops."

"How do you know my name?" Ella asked. "Are you following me, too?"

"No, *mija,* I'm following him." He pointed at Simon; then his voice turned low and urgent. "Listen, both of you, there's no time to argue. I'm not suicidal. I'll keep them busy for a while, then escape via the water. Leave my bike on the same side of the street as your car, keys under the seat. Don't worry about me, think about her."

"But—"

"*Vaya rápidamente. Tenga cuidado,*" Jack said, and without a backward glance, ran toward the ramp where they could all hear the approaching footsteps of the enemy.

As ELLA HAD BEEN in a drugged stupor for the ride out of town, she had no clue how far they'd traveled. It came as a shock to discover they were only a few miles from downtown Tampoo.

She was very careful not to touch Simon's back as she sat behind him. The plaid shirt hid the torn flesh, but the dried blood and glittering glass shards embedded in the cloth suggested some slicing and dicing under the flannel. She'd seen the pain in his eyes as Chopper pushed him down the ramp.

The traffic was still snarled in front of the depot that was now surrounded with police tape and emergency vehicles. Simon stopped short of their destination, guiding the bike to a parking spot a couple of blocks away. She took off the helmet as he turned off the engine, running a shaky hand through her hair. Once she was on her feet again and Simon had deposited the keys, she propped the helmet on the bike seat.

She looked up at him, the world suddenly spinning. In a flash, he grabbed her arms and steadied her and she did what she'd been aching to do for hours. She leaned in against him, tucking her head under his chin, his strong heart thumping under her cheek, the warmth of his body stealing into hers, chasing away the chill. When she felt his lips against her forehead and the pressure of his arms around her, a sense of peace stole into her heart.

The sound of a siren snapped her out of the moment.

"Now what?" she said.

He took her arm and hustled her down the sidewalk toward their car. "I don't suppose you lied to Carl about the contact information?"

"They gave me something. I told them everything." She ran a hand over her face, wincing as she rubbed scratches and abrasions raw again. "Except for the last thing. I lied about the Red Barn."

"Then the meeting isn't at a restaurant?"

"No. It's at a place called Thunder Lodge."

The corner of his lip lifted. "I could have sworn you were telling the truth."

"I hope my father doesn't have to pay for what I did. I can't believe I married Carl. Is it true he planted the bomb in the bus depot?"

"As a diversion to cover snatching you."

"Was anyone hurt?"

"Thankfully it was just me and a kid near the door, and he seemed okay. I'm not sure about anyone else. It must have been a pretty small bomb, but it did a hell of a lot of damage." He rubbed his jaw. "Listen, did you ask the contact any of the questions we talked about? You know, like what the hell is going on?"

"Of course I did. He wouldn't tell me a thing. He actually made the man in Rocky Point seem talkative."

Simon looked away at once.

"Just *who* is Jack?" she asked.

"I was hoping you could tell me. He seemed to know you."

"Everyone seems to know me," she said, and not without some exasperation. "But he said he was following you. Where did he come from?"

"Literally out of the blue. Let's hurry, I don't want to be caught standing on the street if…"

His voice trailed off, but she knew exactly where he was going with it. If Carl and Chopper defeated Jack. If they came looking…

The car was clear of most of the commotion. The knot in Simon's jaw as he looked back at the police directing traffic and the emergency crews investigating the scene tugged at her conscience. What had aligning himself with her cost him? Both personally and professionally, she was sure he was paying an awful price.

Why would a man give up so much of who and what he was for a complete stranger?

The answer seemed very clear—he wouldn't.

But he said he was.

She got into the passenger seat. Within minutes, Simon had circled the block, driving in such a way his back didn't touch the seat. He took the nearest on-ramp to the freeway, which happened to be one heading south, but at this point it didn't seem to matter that much where they went, just that they went. Maybe going the wrong direction for a while was a diversionary tactic.

With a million questions needing answers, they both fell silent, wrapped in their own thoughts.

Ella's eyelids kept closing, her head falling forward until she'd jerk awake. In those few seconds of stolen slumber, dreams pummeled her brain. In an effort to stave off sleep, she stared at Simon. For the first time since meeting him in the hotel lobby, he looked worse than she did. His face and hair were streaked with dried blood, his clothes covered with plaster and dust.

"We've been going southeast for almost an hour," he said. "It's time to loop back around and head north. We need a map. I know where Idaho is, but I don't know where Storm Creek is."

"I don't, either," she said. Her voice sounded thick. For a second, she was back in the depot, heading for the door, anxious to talk to Simon, and then someone had collided with her and she'd turned, and just as she recognized Chopper without a beard, she'd felt a pinprick in her arm and her legs go limp....

She rubbed her arm now, realizing there was a

small irritated patch of skin six inches above her elbow. Man, would she like the opportunity to give Chopper a little of his own medicine!

Simon eventually found a gas station, filled the tank and disappeared into the men's room. When he emerged again, his face and his hair were cleaner, several cuts now bright red against his face. He obviously hadn't tried to take off his shirt, and the spring in his step was subdued. Only the fire in his eyes revealed the anger she sensed inside him.

She'd bought a map and huge cups of coffee while he was gone. As he slid into the car beside her, she showed him the tiny speck in Idaho's panhandle that represented their next destination.

"It's practically in Canada," he said.

"Yes," she agreed, taking small sips of the hot, bitter brew.

They stared at the dot until Simon said, "First things first. The attendant in the station told me where we can trade in this car." He drained his cup as Ella refolded the map, then drove them a mile or two farther, pulling off at an exit promising an airport ahead. Before reaching the airport, he turned off at yet another car rental place. They traveled the rows of cars for a few moments until Simon hit the steering wheel and grinned. "Look," he said.

She looked. "You mean the dark blue truck with the tinted windshield?"

"Yes, but it's not the windshield I'm thinking about, it's the license plate. I was hoping this close to the Washington/Idaho border we might find a vehicle with Idaho plates, and there she is."

"So we won't stand out when we get to Storm Creek."

"Exactly."

"Good plan."

He was gone for almost an hour, but when he reemerged, it was with the keys for the truck. They moved their few careworn belongings, but before he inserted the key in the ignition, Simon paused. "The woman at the counter said Storm Creek is about six or seven driving hours from here," he said. "Before we go another mile, we need to consider the possibility that it may be time to stop this mad chase and turn things over to the police."

She'd known this was coming. Without her wallet and the ID it contained, she couldn't rent a car. She needed Simon's help and yet she was willing to admit it was asking too much. Gazing longingly across the way at a plane taking off from the airport, she said, "I can't buy an airline ticket but I can get on a train. Take me to a station. I understand how hard this all is for you as a policeman. I don't want to keep imposing—"

"Stop," he said, running a hand through his hair. "I don't care about me; this isn't about me."

"Then what's it about?"

"What it's always been about," he said, but then pressed his lips together. "I think we should stay off the main roads. They managed to follow us once before. We can't risk that again."

"Carl said I wasn't innocent in all this. What did he mean?"

"I'm not entirely sure."

"But you suspect something. Was he talking about the man who was murdered in Blue Mountain?"

"I think so," he said reluctantly.

"I wonder if I knew him. Did you?"

"No. And before you ask, I have no idea if you knew him or not. I have no idea if you know any of the older men you're meeting or why you're meeting them or what your father wants. I don't know if you're involved in a murder or if you're a hapless victim."

"I'm involved," she said softly. "I may not have actually killed anyone, but it's obvious I'm in the middle of it all."

"I guess it is," he admitted.

She pressed her fingers against her forehead.

"Carl Baxter and Chopper are dangerous men," Simon said. "They've set off a bomb that could have hurt who knows how many people. At least one man is dead. Not revealing their identities to the cops so they can be apprehended will put more people in harm's way. I can't justify that, even if it hurts you. Do you understand?"

"I think so," she said.

"I have to turn in their names and a description of their vehicle. I have to tell the cops where they're headed so they can be apprehended, which means I'll be leading the cops toward us, too. But thanks to you, they'll be in one part of town and we'll be in another. I'll do it anonymously, but it has to be done. I'll do my best to keep you out of it."

"It's not me I'm worried about. It's my father. He's going to such lengths to make this all a big secret and it seems everyone knows. Am I bringing disaster down upon his head?"

"Regardless of your father's situation—which we don't really know—and your involvement, Carl and Chopper are both dangerous men who have proven they're willing to kill innocent people. We can't stand by and allow them to hurt anyone else."

"You're right, we can't. But you promise me you'll do what you can to keep my father out of harm's way."

"Frankly, it's not your father I'm worried about," he said.

"I know, but do you promise?"

"Yes," he said at last, but he didn't sound happy about it.

Chapter Ten

Simon drove as Ella dozed fitfully beside him. Not familiar with the area, he ended up driving in circles and wasting most of an hour before getting back on the right track. The condition of his back made driving difficult. It would have been a lot easier to take primary instead of secondary highways, and for the entire time it took him to break free of the city, he seemed stalled in one road-construction project after another.

Plus, it was nearly impossible to get comfortable. He knew he needed his back attended to, but he couldn't bear the thought of stopping the truck. He might not see a tail back there, but he could feel one. He wanted the cover of darkness before they stopped.

He couldn't get Jack out of his head, either. Who was he? How did he know Ella, and more to the point, perhaps, how did he know Ella was in trouble? And why did he say he was following

Simon? He flicked his gaze to the rearview mirror, expecting to see a parade back there, but the road was empty of everything except an old converted school bus. Hard to imagine Carl, Chopper or Jack driving that.

Beside him, Ella mumbled incoherently, her head rolling to the side toward the window. Her voice, thick with sleep, was soft but desperate when she mumbled, "No." Her hand fluttered on her lap and then rose to her face. "No!" she repeated.

Her eyes flicked opened and she caught a sob in her throat.

"You okay?" Simon asked, sparing her a long glance.

She swallowed. "Yeah."

He handed her a bottle of water he'd bought at the station when he'd found he couldn't quite get behind coffee. After she took a long drink, she straightened in her seat and looked out at the changing countryside. "Man, how long was I out?"

He glanced at his watch, back now on his own wrist. "Two hours and thirty-three minutes."

"I was dreaming," she said.

"I figured. Your father?"

"Hmm—we were dancing. I was wearing a pink dress and he was twirling me around and then he started to fade, like a ghost, just disappeared into thin air. I was frantic…."

He touched her uninjured hand. Between the two of them, it was getting hard to find an area of skin that wasn't bleeding or bruised. "It was a dream," he murmured.

"It was so real. Oh, Simon, I don't know what to do. What if the police want him? What if he, I don't know, robbed a bank for instance? Maybe that's why he fled the U.S.A. and moved to Canada."

"We have extradition agreements with Canada. He couldn't evade the U.S. law in Canada."

"Maybe he's hiding. Or maybe he did something else that wasn't illegal, just immoral."

"We'll find out tomorrow," he said firmly.

She stopped fussing, going as far as flashing him a smile. "I get tied up in knots."

"I don't blame you."

She narrowed her eyes as she studied him. Then he heard her sigh. "I'm also selfish. I forgot how hurt you are. Stop the truck."

"What—"

"Stop it. Right now." He pulled over to the side of the road as the old bus rumbled by them. "Change seats, I'm driving," she said. To punctuate her intent, she opened her door and came around to his side of the truck. Opening the door, she added, "Out."

Very gingerly, he got out of the truck, his back raging with fire. She took his place behind the wheel. "I'm driving to a motel and I'm taking care of your back."

"We should wait for dark—"

"We shouldn't have waited at all, I should have insisted earlier. Get in." Once he'd climbed into the passenger seat, she pulled onto the highway. He sat sideways, his left arm against the back of the seat. Without driving to concentrate on, he felt his back start to burn.

They passed a sign announcing a city up ahead. "We'll stop there," she said.

"Somewhere seedy and way off the beaten track," he told her.

"That goes without saying. I have a plan, trust me."

He smiled. The sleep had done her good. She glanced at him and grinned, laughing a little, shaking her head. It was a familiar gesture, and for some reason, it lodged in his heart. All that was missing was the mass of gold curls that used to dance as she moved.

Oh, God, he wasn't still harboring hope for her—for *them*—was he?

It was as though she read his mind. She said, "Tell me why you broke the mermaid's heart."

He shrugged and wished he hadn't, because it hurt like blazes. "We grew apart," he said.

"Explain that."

"Well, she wanted one thing and I wanted another."

"Do you always talk in circles like this?"

"She hated me being in law enforcement, for instance."

"Smart girl."

"Why do you say that?"

"It's dangerous work, right? Maybe she wanted to have babies, maybe she didn't want their father to be killed arresting some sleazeball."

Had her memory returned? Was she messing with him? He stared at her exquisite profile as he responded, "Or maybe she was running from something."

She smiled. "That's more exciting," she said. "I like that better."

He saw no subterfuge in the glance she cast his way.

"So you broke up with her."

"Well, maybe it was a little more mutual than that," he said. "She'd been keeping secrets and when I pressed her for details she blew up and called me a prying bastard."

"What did you call her?"

"Secretive. Controlling."

"Ouch. So now there's no more you and her. That's very sad, Simon."

"Yes, it is," he said.

They entered the town of Twilight around dinnertime. It appeared to be a small town with lots of empty buildings, the kind of thing that tended to happen when a major highway bypassed a city. Simon spied a telephone booth in the overgrown parking lot of a long-closed miniature golf course. "Pull in there, park behind those trees. I've got to call a friend."

She did as he asked, getting out of the truck at the same time he did. When he reached the phone booth he looked back to see she'd wandered over to the fence surrounding the unkempt golf course, and was staring in at the old windmills and clowns that had once delighted children.

Though the booth didn't have a telephone directory any longer, the phone itself had a dial tone, and that brought a sigh of relief. Devin took the collect call. From the background clatter, he was either washing dishes or fixing dinner. "Glad you called," he said. "Guess what? Robert Connors was a retired policeman from guess where?"

"Chicago, like Jerry Bucker?"

"Exactly."

"Then Connors's murder is related to all this."

"It has to be. He has to be the old guy your girl met at the restaurant, which means other than the murderer, she's the last to see him alive, and there is a roomful of witnesses to identify her. The cops are going to want to question her."

Simon leaned his forehead against the glass panel of the booth. "I phoned in an anonymous tip to the police today about the identity of the men I think are responsible for the deaths of Bucker and Connors. When this is all over, hopefully tomorrow, I'll get back to Blue Mountain and go see the chief."

"He'll have your head. Withholding information, aiding and abetting—"

"Please, don't read me the list. I knew what I was doing when I took sides a couple of days ago. I just have to make sure Ella is innocent before those two spill their guts and try to blame everything on her. I can't take the chance she winds up in prison."

"Now, wait a second," Devin said with a rattle of pans that announced his inattention to what he was doing on the home front. "I thought you broke up with this girl. Why can't you let her go?"

Simon hadn't told Devin about Ella's pregnancy. He wasn't going to tell anyone other than his cousin until Ella remembered on her own or he broke down and told her himself.

Devin whistled. "You still have feelings for her."

Simon acknowledged as much. There was no

denying—or quantifying—that fact. He had feelings for her, feelings that were beginning to make him doubt everything, but this wasn't the time to worry about it.

"Listen to me," Devin said. "I can't find her maiden name, but I know I've got to be getting close. Without a legal name change, however, her marriage to Carl Baxter might very well be invalid. But it might not."

"Let's take things one disaster at a time," Simon said.

"Speaking of disasters in the making, there was some guy asking around about you. Dark, speaks with a slight Spanish accent. Know him?"

"Kind of," Simon said.

After hearing that so far Devin hadn't been grilled by the cops, he hung up.

He wanted to call Virginia but didn't dare. He couldn't risk involving her and there really wasn't anything new she could offer. She'd told him to let Ella's memory come back on its own and it seemed to be happening. What they needed was time. What they didn't have was time.

Ella had memories of a mother and father now, and a brother, all two-dimensional figures moving through her dreams and sometimes stealing into her waking thoughts. He couldn't help but wonder who would be next. He could tell she suspected him of having prior knowledge of her—he thought it likely only the string of worsening circumstances kept her from really pressing the issue.

He walked back to the fence, his back in such pain it was hard to think straight. She was staring at a giant plaster bear balanced on top of a white flower. The bear wore lederhosen and held a giant beer stein in one hand. Its mouth was wide open as though it was yodeling.

"What are you looking at?" he asked as he put his fingers through the wire next to Ella's.

She leaned her head against the fence and gazed up at him. "A bird has built a nest in the bear's mouth. Listen."

He didn't hear anything until a small black-and-gray bird swooped over his head and landed on one of the bear's yellow teeth, setting off a cacophony of high-pitched cheeps from the hatchlings inside the nest.

"Starlings," he said softly. "The scourge of American songbirds."

"Starlings," she repeated slowly as though tasting the word. "Starlings. Why are they the scourge of American songbirds?"

"They're not a native bird. They drive out other birds, even destroy eggs."

"How do you know all this?"

"My mom and dad have several acres. They

love their birds. Want to hear about the innocent-looking but highly destructive house sparrow?"

She laughed, but then her eyes grew gentle. He loved it when she looked at him that way. In the past it had been an invitation for intimacy, not just sex, but a letting down of her formidable guard, a sign she was feeling safe and would allow him to get a little closer. His gaze dipped down to her waist and the small curve of her belly.

The thought her baby might not be his baby just about unhinged him. He wrapped his fingers around hers and looked deep into her eyes.

She didn't move, but her focus shifted to his mouth as their heads drifted together. A million remembered sensations coursed through his body as his lips touched hers.

In an instant, as her lips parted, he was whisked away to the night they first met. She, draped in a million shades of blue and green, skin sparkling with glitter, eyes so big and trusting he'd been mesmerized the moment he walked into the club and saw her standing alone. By the end of the night, they'd kissed a hundred times. By the end of the weekend, they'd been lovers.

He'd thought to build a future with her despite his mother's warnings about Ella's reserve. And now as her warm mouth and silken tongue merged with his, he thought that way again. He yearned to wrap her in his arms and back her against the fence, take what she was offering, make her his one more time.

He straightened up as, above them, the baby birds welcomed their mother or father back to the nest. He ran a finger over her lips. If she was willing, he was willing; why pretend he wasn't?

"For a moment there, I remembered what sex was like," she whispered, "and I wanted to have it again, right here, right now, with you."

"What a wonderful idea," he whispered against her cheek.

She looked down at her left hand. "I'm a married woman."

"Ella—"

"Even if the marriage is over, the fact is I was with him when we had the accident. He knew to expect the contact in the restaurant. In my mind, that means we were in 'it' together and a man is dead. I can still hear him saying I'm not innocent, and somehow, I think I believe him, I think he's right."

"You don't know any of this."

"And then there's Jack, showing up out of nowhere but knowing my name, and cautioning against calling the police…. Just how many men do I know? Are they all lovers or have they been in the past?"

Good questions. Simon stared into her eyes. "I don't know."

"I can see that. But you do know more about me than you're telling."

"Yes," he said. "Let me be honest. My cousin is a doctor. She said ideally, you should go home and come to your memories through familiar things. She called it associational therapy."

Ella took a deep breath. "I've always felt that's the way it should have happened. I've been wondering ever since I realized I can't trust Carl if he warped what the hospital doctors said, if he just told me what suited him. Maybe the doctors never intended me to have to go through this in this way."

"Maybe you're right. And maybe in a perfect world, you could go home. There're just a few little catches."

"My father needs me," she said firmly.

That hadn't been the catch he was thinking of. He'd been thinking more along the lines of the dead men, a bomb and her possible involvement.

And yet she'd left her houselights burning and the snow globe—he was almost positive she'd been taken against her will. Did that mean she hadn't wanted to help her father or that she'd planned to help him all along and Carl Baxter showed up or she and Carl were in cahoots from the beginning but had a falling-out?

She'd been acting strange, she'd been keeping secrets. Was it Carl or her father or both?

"You look as confused as I feel," Ella said softly. As he'd been mulling things over, she'd slipped her wedding ring off her finger. "Well, I may be married to the jerk, but I don't have to wear his ring, do I?" And with that, she tossed the gold band through the fence, where it disappeared into the brush. She smiled fleetingly and added, "You're in such pain. Get in the truck."

"No sex right here on the ground?" he said only half jokingly.

"With your back full of glass?"

"You could be on the bottom."

She shook her head. "Get in the truck." She took one last look at the nest up inside the bear's mouth. "Bye, little starlings," she said, drawing out their name.

Back in take-charge mode, she dropped him off at a motel so disreputable they were both pretty sure the rooms rented by the hour. Then, against his protests, she drove off with assurances she would park the truck in the parking lot of a different motel she'd passed a few blocks away. He rented them a room and awaited her return with acid burning his throat.

But she did return, her step more full of vigor than he'd seen it so far, the very act of taking control seeming to empower her. Once again, he thought of the Ella he'd grown to know—the woman who could take care of just about everything.

She moved the two plug-in lamps in the dingy room near a chair she'd set up next to the bathroom door, angling their shades for light. He sat on a chair with his arms hooked over the rungs, his back exposed, as she peeled away his clothes. She was trying to be gentle, he knew that, but by now the blood had caked around the glass shards and the pain was excruciating.

"Oh, ack!" she said as she cut away the last piece of his clothing. Good thing he'd bought scissors when he'd bought antiseptic and bandages. "You're a mess."

"Less chatter, more work," he said, his breathing shallow. "There are tweezers in the bag, too."

"I have them. You want something to bite on?"

"No, thanks. Just get it over with."

The next few minutes passed in near silence as one by one, she located and extracted the splinters. When she muttered she'd gotten them all, she filled the sink with warm, sudsy water and carefully rinsed his skin. He almost jumped off the chair when the washcloth caught on a piece of glass she'd missed, but that was soon out, as well.

By the time she'd bathed his back and dried it, applied ointments and bandages and he'd found a clean shirt in his duffel, they were both frazzled but hungry for dinner and for information. But first Ella insisted on taking a shower, so while she lathered up behind a closed door, he lay on the bed on his stomach and prayed for the aspirin to kick in.

Thirty minutes later, they left the room carrying all their belongings, the key back on the dresser.

The truck was as Ella had left it, though they did hide out across the street in a Laundromat watching for signs of Carl or Chopper before approaching it. When it was obviously all clear, they drove to a fast food restaurant, where they both ordered chicken sandwiches and milkshakes. It was the first time he'd seen Ella eat fast food.

While dining in the truck, they studied the road map for the best route into Idaho. A long night of driving loomed ahead.

"There's a light on down the block, and from the size of the building, I'm betting it's city hall," he announced as he folded the map.

"What's at city hall?"

"Well, a newsstand probably, maybe someone who heard about the bombing. I can't go to the police department for information and I don't know where else to start to get answers, so let's try city hall."

He drove the few blocks down the road and parked on a side street. A sign directly in front of them announced the adjoining library, which turned out to be a small wing of the city building. It was open two nights a week and tonight was one of them. "We're in luck," he said.

"Closing time in twenty-five minutes," Ella noted as they approached the door.

The library might be compact, but it was connected to the Internet. After showing his driver's license, Simon was allotted time on the computer and immediately typed in *Tampoo, WA bomb.*

'Two Injured in Depot Bombing,' announced the headline, and Simon sighed with relief. No deaths. One ten-year-old boy taken to emergency and released, one elderly woman held in the hospital for observation, no leads, which meant his anonymous phone call to the cops giving them Carl Baxter's name hadn't reached the press yet. Simon leaned back in the chair for an instant, then sat ramrod straight. Damn back.

He turned to tell Ella the good news, but she was standing several feet away staring at a poster of birds that was apparently part of the library décor.

As though she felt his gaze upon her, she turned to face him. Her expression caught his attention and he began to stand. Before he could get to his feet, she had crossed the small room and pulled a chair up next to his.

"His name is Starling," she said softly.

"What do you mean his name is Starling? Whose name is Starling?"

"My father."

"Are you sure?"

"The minute you told me what those birds were called, I felt something."

"Like what?"

"I don't know. A feeling of familiarity, maybe. And then when I looked at the poster and saw the word *Starling* in print, I knew. That's my father's name. Starling."

"Not Thorton. That name rings no familiar bells?"

"Thorton? No, why?"

"Because that's the name you used when you married Carl Baxter."

"How do you know this?"

"I have a friend who's a private investigator. He's trying to find out anything he can about you and Carl and Chopper and even your father. We need help if we're going to live through this and if we're going to help your dad."

She stared at him a second before slowly nodding. "Yes, of course."

"Starling, huh?" he repeated. He'd never heard her called that before. Of course, he'd never heard the name Thorton, either, or, for that matter, about a marriage, or a father. Her brother had apparently died tragically a year or so ago—she must have been dealing with his loss when they started dating and yet she'd never said a word.

"Why would I have a different name than my father before I was even married?" she asked.

Several possibilities occurred to him: she'd been married before; this father she remembered with such tenderness was a stepfather; her parents had never married; maybe even she'd gone to jail and had taken a new name upon release. All useless speculation.

Glancing at the computer screen, he said, "I could type Starling in, see what we get."

She stood abruptly. "I don't know."

"What are you afraid of?" he asked gently.

"Isn't it obvious?"

"No—"

"Are nice, normal people on the Internet? Isn't it mainly people who have made a name for themselves in some way? People who have, you know, done something hideous?"

"Or wonderful or notable or public—"

"I don't want to know," she insisted, and he could tell from the tilt of her chin that her mind was made up. "Please understand, I just can't." And with that she turned on her heel and hurried out of the library.

What now? He couldn't let her wander around town alone where she might be sighted. She was just anxious enough that she might not use her head. On the other hand, she had the keys to the truck and she knew the stakes and he was itching to type *Starling* into the computer....

"Ten minutes, sir," the librarian told him in a soft voice. He was the only patron left in the building. He nodded at her and typed in *Starling*.

Dozens of links to birds popped up on the screen. He scrolled through them quickly, moving on to lists of organizations and businesses, music groups and actors and finally *Starling, Tyler.*

He clicked on the link and went immediately to an archived article on a Chicago cop named Tyler Starling written over fifteen years before.

The librarian was quietly walking through the aisles, preparing for closing. He knew she wanted time to clear off the desk at which he sat, so he read as fast as he could, ignoring tempting links to other sites and possible further explanations.

And what he read started to explain a whole lot about Ella, about what was going on, and about the depth of the danger they faced.

But not everything.

He froze as another thought surfaced. He'd sent the police to Storm Creek to look for Carl Baxter and Chopper, and that's where Ella's father was planning a secret rendezvous with his daughter. What would happen if the police caught on to

Ella's father's identity? It was true they would be in different parts of town, but Storm Creek was the smallest of dots on the map.

The whole thing was a giant recipe for disaster and he'd had more than a little bit to do with creating it.

Ella would hate him forever if he didn't figure out a way to make this all work out.

Chapter Eleven

The sandwich that had tasted pretty good an hour before now was the eye of the hurricane brewing in Ella's stomach. She sat in the dark truck waiting for Simon's return, wishing he'd hurry and yet also wishing he'd never come back because she had a feeling she wasn't going to like what he found on the Internet.

She put a hand over her stomach and closed her eyes, willing the food to stay where it belonged. This was the first time she'd had nausea at night. Usually it was the morning—

Her eyes popped open.

Nausea in the morning.

No, it couldn't be, but her memory took her right back to the morning she'd tried on pants and found that although they fit her everywhere else, they were too tight in the waist. Both hands went to her breasts. Were they sensitive? Yes!

A knock on the window sent her scrambling to

open the driver's door for Simon. He got into the truck slowly, carefully, sliding into the seat as though very mindful of his back.

"You want me to drive?" she asked.

"No. Give me a second to find a semi-comfortable position. I don't think we'd better risk an unlicensed driver at this point, do you?"

"Probably not," she said.

"Do you want to know what I found?" he asked as she handed him the keys. He inserted the right one in the ignition, but he didn't start the engine.

"Am I going to like it?"

"No."

The nausea rose up her throat. "Then let's wait. I need a bathroom. Now."

He started the truck and drove back to the fast food restaurant, where Ella bolted inside, making it just in time to lose her dinner in the privacy of a stall. She washed out her mouth, splashed water on her face and returned to the truck feeling slightly better.

Pregnant.

What if the nausea wasn't because of the concussion? What if it wasn't because of medication, which she hadn't taken in days anyway? What if it was because she was pregnant?

Which begged the question: Who was the father?

Jack? Was that how he knew her? Carl Baxter? Someone else?

And what about all the drugs she'd been given at the hospital and the truth serum or whatever it was Chopper stuck her with at the bus depot?

"Ella?"

She startled. Simon was staring at her, his gray eyes wide with concern. "Are you okay? What's wrong?"

"Dinner didn't sit so good. Guess it's been a rough day. Besides, I'm worried about my dad." She added that last part because it was the one overriding truth of her life right now. She loved her father. She needed her father.

Simon nodded once and started the truck again. A few minutes later they were rolling out of Twilight on their way to Idaho, the world reduced to the wedge of light illuminated by the headlamps.

She didn't want to talk to Simon and yet she did. Good heavens, she had to talk to someone, she couldn't carry news like this by herself.

If it was true.

Maybe it wasn't, but if it was, then there was one plea she would offer up to whatever stray gods might be looking out for her: *don't let Carl Baxter be the father....*

Her hands bunched into fists in her lap. She wanted to pound her head against the door until it spilled its secrets. All the reasons and the explanations and answers and knowledge were right there inside her and yet walled off. Her empty stomach gurgled and spat.

As much as she hated to admit it, she was worried what conclusions Simon might reach when he heard she might be pregnant. Would he assume Carl was the father?

She couldn't imagine rolling around naked with Carl. Couldn't imagine wanting him the way she'd wanted Simon all day. Stroking him. Loving him. Unbelievable.

"Ella," Simon said, and once again, she'd been so caught up in her tangled thoughts the sound of his voice caused her to jerk.

"What?"

He patted her hand. "I know how worried you are about your father."

"My father. Yes, I'm worried about my father."

"I think I found him on the Internet."

She nodded into the dark. "I had a feeling. Go ahead, it must be pretty bad if you're so worried about telling me it."

"It is pretty bad. He may not be the man you think he is."

"What do you mean?"

"He may not be the kind of man you'd want as a dad. It seems he—"

"Just a minute," she snapped. "I thought I was

ready to hear it, but I'm not. My father is the only reality I have right now and what I can remember of him is wonderful. Don't take that away from me unless you are absolutely positive the Starling you read about is my father."

He was quiet for several minutes. "I'm not positive," he finally said. "It seems likely, but without knowing your past, it's hard for me to say."

"Then don't tell me."

"Okay."

She sat in silence as the miles droned on. Her hands clenched and unclenched, straying to her midsection whenever she wasn't thinking about them.

A baby.

She'd always wanted a baby.

How did she know that? Maybe she'd never wanted children. And with her father being so terribly important to her, how could she face bringing a child into the world without knowing who his or her father was? How did she deny her child a father?

She glanced over at Simon, who was making a big deal of not looking at her. If she was free to name a father for her baby, it would be him. He was big, but gentle. He was strong. He took care of people even if he was a policeman. He'd taken care of her from the moment he rescued her off the face of the bluff. He'd stood by her.

And he was the only man she really knew at the moment.

Besides, he was hot.

She smiled to herself, happy for the cover of darkness. He'd make a wonderful father for any baby, and a wonderful husband, too. She thought back to the moment when they'd stared at each other by the fence, to the feeling of his lips touching hers, his beard rough against her cheek, his intensity that had burned down to her shoes and filled her head with a kaleidoscope of images and impressions.

Then later, washing his back, her fingers brushing his hot skin, her eyes devouring the muscles in his shoulders and arms. She swallowed hard. If she was pregnant, then she'd already decided about a father for her child. There was no choice. The decision was already made and it wasn't Simon Task.

But maybe it was someone whom she admired and lusted after just as much. Surely her memory would return long before she gave birth and it needn't reveal Carl Baxter as her lover.

Maybe it was Jack. There was no doubt he was a very good-looking man with his tanned skin and long black hair, those light eyes and the velvet softness of his voice.

But he wasn't Simon....

Maybe she wasn't even pregnant. Maybe she was just spinning dreams.

Dreams. Maybe that's all she had. Maybe that's all she would ever have. She closed her eyes as she rested her head against the window. The miles sped beneath the tires. She tried to remember her last dream, or at least the beginning of it. The pink dress. The music. Her father. She could see herself looking up at him, way up, forever up, and there was never a face, no way of telling what he looked like, just his hands gripping hers and the music, and the spinning…

And then, again, he was gone, and she was still spinning, hands stretched out in front, but older now, no longer wearing pink, her hair long and floating, white, like clouds, like starlight. In her father's place was now a woman who reached out and caught Ella's hands and pulled her to a stop. A woman slapping her face, tears welling in her eyes, tears running down her cheeks…

Ella gasped and choked and sputtered, coming to her senses with ragged breaths and a hammering heart.

It was very dark and quiet. She sat there alone, catching her breath, not entirely sure she wasn't still dreaming.

Two lights appeared. It took Ella a moment to identify them as headlights on a big truck pulling into the same large area in which Simon had parked. In the instant the headlights illuminated the interior of the truck, her mind took a mental snapshot.

Simon sleeping, the dark stubble of his beard blending into the shadows, handsome beyond enduring. He was braced behind the steering wheel kind of funny so his back wouldn't touch the seat. She could hear the sound of his breathing, heavy and deep and regular as though he was so exhausted neither lights nor crying women could rouse him from slumber.

Here by herself in the very quiet dark, she could admit something very private: she was falling for him.

The truck pulled into a space a few cars over. It must be a rest stop they were in, or a park of some kind. But where? The only thing she was certain of was that she didn't want to wake Simon. Not only did he need the sleep as he had to do all the driving, but she didn't want to talk to him right now, either.

However, sleeping was next to impossible. Not only had she already slept for hours, but her stomach was alternately empty and sick and her hand throbbed, probably because she'd had to tug to get the ring off. Every time she tried to get comfortable, something new hurt, and if she just sat still, her thoughts wandered back to dreams of her father and the crying woman.

Her mother, that's who that woman was. Crying. Slapping Ella. Ella crying.

Good heavens, what had happened in her past? Could Simon telling her about it be any worse than reliving it one miserable dream after the other?

SIMON AWOKE with the first morning light to find Ella staring at him.

He relaxed, wincing as his back touched the seat but staying still until the worst of the pain subsided. It hurt less today although he felt lethargic, probably to be expected given the past few days.

"You been awake long?" he mumbled.

"Not long."

If he looked half as worn out and beat up as she did, they were in trouble. What they were going through was a more personal battle than anything he'd ever faced aboard ship in the navy, its outcome just as unpredictable as any war.

"Where are we?" she asked.

He rubbed his eyes and covered a yawn with a fist. "About ten miles past the place I should have stopped last night because my eyes kept drifting shut. It's a county park of some kind. There are no official rest stops off these little highways we're using. Let me walk around a bit and wash my face and we can get going."

"I'll join you," she said.

As she moved around the truck, he noticed the way her hand brushed her stomach and that made him notice the slight bump against her clothes. He looked away so she wouldn't see him staring.

They stretched their legs by walking down to a small river, used the minimal restrooms to freshen up, and met back at the truck a few minutes later, where they both stood for a moment, letting the sun bathe their faces.

"Are you hungry?" he said.

"Not really."

"I could use coffee."

"Simon, how far are we from Storm Creek?"

"A couple of hours. But I forgot to look up Thunder Lodge last night at the library, and that could be way outside of town. We need to hit another computer."

She nodded briefly. "If you look for additional references to the man you think is my father, are you likely to find them?"

"Absolutely."

"Could you find enough to know for sure this Starling you've found is really my dad?"

"I think so. If I can find an article that includes information about his family, it might mention you."

"What's this man's first name?"

"Tyler."

"And Susan," she said, tossing the word out as

though it had been sitting on the edge of her tongue waiting to take flight. "Susan," she repeated.

"Your mother?"

"Yes."

"So the Tyler—"

"I don't know about Tyler, I just know Susan and I didn't even know I knew that until thirty seconds ago. But that could help, right?"

"Yes."

"Then we need to drive until we get to a city large enough to have a library."

"Okay," he said, and with this as their plan, they both got back into the truck.

"How's your back?" she asked him as he slid in behind the wheel.

"Not too bad. How are all your aches and wounds?"

"Not too bad," she said, and they smiled at each other.

The winding road out of the park was bordered by blossoming fruit trees. It was a windy day, so there were drifts of pale petals floating in the air, almost like snow. Simon darted glances Ella's way, but she seemed introverted this morning.

He'd seen her that way before, of course, and as they hit the highway again, he thought back to the times she'd grown distant and tried to relate them to a common thread. The last time had been at his parents' house where they'd gone for his father's sixtieth birthday party. His father had been delighted with Ella's gift of homemade cashew brittle and he'd spontaneously hugged her. Ella had withdrawn almost at once, pulling into herself, retreating.

That had been the moment Simon had begun to seriously contemplate the possibility that Ella didn't fit into his life very well, that for over a year, he'd been fitting himself into hers but there hadn't been much give-and-take.

And now he knew she had a thing about fathers, a difficult past with hers that had probably made the spontaneous show of affection from his dad unbearably uncomfortable.

Was that when she'd begun to get even more secretive? Had she made up her mind that night to drive him away or had Carl paid her a visit or had seeing his dad made her remember her own? Maybe she'd called him when she returned home, maybe that's what set all this in motion.

Face it. If Tyler Starling was her father, he was a crook and a murderer.

How did Simon tell Ella this and yet how did he let her keep risking her life for such a man? Undoubtedly, she had unresolved feelings about him and if her memories were progressing from the distant past to the present, sooner or later she would stumble across her true feelings. Was it better for her to discover that on her own?

How did he know?

And there was another thing that stung him more than he liked to admit and that was that she hadn't trusted him enough to talk about her past. It was pretty clear Carl Baxter knew about her dad—so why hadn't she told Simon? Was it an indication of how little she thought he could handle? Was it because he was a cop?

"Sure you don't want anything to eat?" he said. She glanced at him with a little of the old uneasiness flickering behind her blue irises. "Are you feeling okay?" he added.

"I feel fine," she said so quickly the words tumbled together.

"Your stomach isn't bothering you?"

"No," she said firmly, and looked out the window.

He turned his attention to the road.

Boy, the old Ella was coming back with a vengeance. He smiled to himself, kind of glad. The sweeter version had been just that—more compliant, easier to talk to, sweeter. But this was his Ella. Kind of touchy.

Wait a second.

He glanced her way again. Her hand was hovering near her stomach area.

Suddenly he understood why she was acting

different. *She knew.* She'd figured it out and she didn't want to tell him.

She knew or suspected she was pregnant, so she was going to pretend she felt no nausea and everything was fine so she didn't have to discuss it.

Yeah, well, he hadn't exactly been up front with her, had he? And did he want to talk about a baby with her, a baby he was hoping was his, when he'd sworn he'd never met her before a few days ago? *Uh, no.*

"Aren't you going to stop for coffee?" she said as they rolled by signs announcing Coeur d'Alene.

"No. We'll bypass this city. Too big. Look at the map and see if there's a smaller town nearby. With Internet connection, it doesn't really matter how big a library is anymore."

She wrangled with the map for a few minutes. "Several miles ahead. Off to the left, a little place called Sellers. We ought to be there right around the time the library opens."

Eventually, they pulled off into Sellers, a town with a wholesome if isolated feel to it. While Simon filled the gas tank, Ella asked the attendant for directions to the library.

This time it was a new building, spacious with room to grow. Skylights overhead let in dappled sun; comfortable chairs held reading patrons. There was a whole bank of computers with several unused this time of day. The reference librarian studied Simon's driver's license for a few moments before allowing them both the use of a computer.

"You look up Thunder Lodge, I'll find out about Tyler Starling," Simon said. He noticed Ella took a machine angled so she couldn't see his screen. Her reluctance to know the truth about her father left him a little confused, but he let that go as he reconnected with the site he'd searched the night before.

It was a Chicago newspaper and the headlines were huge. Starling Steals Money and Runs. Simon quickly reread what he'd seen the night before, this time following links to other sites and articles detailing the depth of Starling's depravity, the manhunt, the condemnations from fellow officers right up to the commissioner, all repeating over and over again that Tyler Starling betrayed the public trust. He was a thief, a criminal, a murderer, and he would stand trial. Justice would be served.

He was never caught.

Looking for references to Tyler Starling's family, Simon kept searching. He about fell off his chair when he saw the man's wife's name: Susan. The children weren't named, but there were two of them, a boy of twenty and a girl of twelve at the time of the scandal.

He connected with another site that turned out

to be an obituary for Susan Starling dated four years later. There was a graveside photo in a following article. It revealed a very pale young girl standing next to an ornate headstone.

The girl stood alone.

Short brown hair as she had now, blue eyes. Ella. Younger, yes. But Ella.

He felt a hand on his shoulder and jumped, peering up to see Ella looking down at him. "I need some change to make copies of the directions to Thunder…"

Her voice trailed off as something of what he'd just seen must have registered on his face. Her gaze dipped down to the screen. Simon fought the urge to hit the keys that would send the photograph into cyberspace.

As he sat there pinned between the computer and Ella, she read the caption under the photo aloud.

"Eleanor Starling visits her mother's grave."

Sensing her shock, Simon turned the swivel chair in time to catch her, wincing when her arm fell against his back. She was chalky white as she sat on his lap, her eyes filling with tears.

"She used to hit me," Ella said, and Simon swore he heard a young girl speaking and not this beautiful, strong woman. He put his arms around her. "She was mean."

"I'm sorry," Simon said. He hit a key to send the

photo away, unsure what to do next. They needed the printouts if they were to make the meeting in a timely manner, but maybe she'd give it up now. Maybe now that she remembered a mother who abused her, she would recall the crimes her father had run from and decide to hell with him.

"Do you still want to get directions?" he asked softly.

She stared into his eyes for a moment, then nodded.

"Can you stand?"

She stood quickly as if to prove her resiliency. He got to his feet, ready to grab her if she ran.

He had the feeling she'd been running for the better part of sixteen years.

Chapter Twelve

"Do you want to talk about it?" Simon asked.

She shook her head. She didn't know what to say; she couldn't even dredge up an emotion past sadness. The beatings had happened, but it was as though they'd happened to someone else or to characters in a book.

"I'm sorry, Ella."

She nodded, still too shocked by the realization that her mother had abused her to process Simon's remarks. She knew she had to snap out of it, but while her brain had been blank to the point of distraction for days, it was now filled with fleeting images too hazy to decipher. And voices! Urgent whispers banged against each other. She put a hand on either side of her head and closed her eyes.

She knew she should be brave enough to ask Simon the rest of what he knew. About her father. About her mother's death. Instead she wanted to open the truck door and fling herself away from him, away from the voices, away from everything.

"Ella," Simon said. "Ella!"

She unclasped her head and opened her eyes.

"I'm taking you back to Blue Mountain," he said. "You're not going through this anymore."

"I have to," she whispered.

"No, you don't," he said. "Trust me, your father isn't worth it."

"That doesn't change anything," she said softly. Simon's voice seemed to have stilled the others in her head and she silently pleaded with him to keep talking.

He cast her an impatient glance. "How can you say that?"

"Because it doesn't. I have to see this through. For my mother. For my father. Hell, as far as I know, for my dead brother."

"What if I told you your father is wanted for murder?"

She swallowed hard and tried to think clearly. She finally said, "He's still my father. He helped me when I was little. I adored him and now he needs me."

"And you still want to help him even though he's wanted for murder?"

"Was he convicted?"

"He never stood trial. He ran away from the law and away from your family."

"It doesn't change anything. My father is the one real thing in my life. I'm here to save him, I know that in my heart. That's about all I know." She paused for a second before adding, "Why are you here, Simon?"

"Because of you," he said slowly. They were on a small road, the countryside around them growing increasingly wooded and remote.

"That's what you keep saying," she said. "But it doesn't really make much sense. You're risking everything for me. Why would you do that?"

He was silent for over a mile until he finally cleared his throat, looking at her briefly before he began speaking, then keeping his gaze on the road where it needed to be.

"Do you remember me telling you about the woman I loved?"

"Yes."

"Maybe I didn't mention how quickly it happened."

"What do you mean?"

"How quickly I fell for her. Almost immediately, in fact. I'm like that with women. No second-guessing, no *ifs* and *ands*, I just know."

"Wait a second," she said slowly. "Are you trying to tell me you've fallen in love with me?"

That earned her another quick glance. "That's what I'm trying to tell you, yes."

"And that's why you're risking life and limb and career."

"It makes me sound like an idiot when you put it that way," he said.

"How would you put it, then?"

He thought for a second before saying, "I guess I'm an idiot."

She smiled at his profile. She didn't believe him, not for a single moment. Her hands had settled on her abdomen as they were so likely to do lately, as though she knew without proof there was a life growing inside her. She couldn't tell Simon about the baby, especially when she wasn't positive there even was one, and yet the possibility of that child was the reason she had to see her father.

Anyway, Simon was keeping secrets of his own. There was more going on here than he wanted to say, but he'd already told her about his cousin's warnings to let her come to these conclusions herself, so she decided to let him off the hook.

If nothing else, the exchange of words had cleared the voices and images out of her head, and she sat back now, taking a deep breath.

"What did you find out about Thunder Lodge?" Simon asked.

Happy to move along to a different subject, as well, she paraphrased the printout.

"Thunder Lodge was a privately owned campground back in the fifties. Some kind of legal hassle between warring heirs closed it down and it never truly recovered. Now only a few of the buildings are kept up and rented out during the summer for private functions. There's a river there and a waterfall called, guess what?"

"Thunder Falls?"

"Very good. 'Peaceful, remote, tranquil and serene' are a few of the adjectives they use." Peaceful and serene. The words sounded like impossible dreams.

"How far is it from the Canadian border?" Simon queried.

"It's actually right on it. There's a border crossing in a nearby town, but I gather Thunder Falls forms a natural barrier." She paused for a second before adding, "It sounds like an awfully remote place to meet, doesn't it?"

"Very. But your father is a man on the run."

"I get the feeling this is it, though, you know what I mean? I can't imagine we're coming all the way up here just to go farther."

"We can't go to Canada," he said as they entered the city limits of another small town. "We don't have passports." He stopped to pull on the

knit hat. One glance in the mirror alarmed him—
the beard was too long, too noticeable.

"We need to stop," he said. They had three hours
to reach Thunder Lodge, which was only twenty
miles away now. They hadn't eaten all day and both
of them needed to be ready for whatever came next.

Once again they rented a cheap motel room,
then walked half a block to a deli, where Simon
bought and consumed a pastrami on rye and Ella
picked at a grape and feta salad. Then they walked
back to the motel, her stride finally strong again,
keeping up with his. He wasn't sure how Ella was
feeling about him right now, but he knew how he
felt about her and it was disconcerting.

He didn't want to feel anything for her. He
knew he cared about her welfare and that of the
baby, but caring for her as a woman, as his
woman, well, that was just plain nuts. The fact
was, however, he was growing increasingly aware
of her again, just as he had been the first time he
fell in love with her.

He told himself to knock it off and keep his
mind on the mess they were in. It would all be over
in a couple of hours.

But once inside the room, she pulled her tunic
over her head, revealing a skintight white T-shirt
with a deep-scooped neck. The knit hugged her
breasts and rose and fell as she breathed. Seem-

ingly oblivious of what the sight of her half dressed did to him, she sat on the side of the bed and took off her shoes and socks, revealing trim ankles he knew all too well evolved into long, curved legs and from there to a body that was ripe and soft and lean at the same time.

He found himself itching to help her undress, curious what her naked belly looked like with a budding pregnancy cradled within. He wanted to lay his hand on her bare skin, over the developing child he hoped was his…

"I'll take the first shower," he said abruptly, and closed the door behind himself. Snap out of it! First he shaved off the beard, then climbed into the shower, cringing for a few seconds as the spray hit his back. Afterward, he emerged into the bedroom to find Ella ready with bandages and antibiotics.

She wore the T-shirt with her sweatpants, and though she was fully clothed, naked images of her ran rampant in his head.

"Sit down," she said, gesturing at the bed, and he did so. She climbed onto the mattress behind him, perched on her knees. Her touch started fires wherever her fingers lingered as she checked the wounds on his back. When she leaned forward, her hair brushed the side of his face, her breath warmed his skin, her breasts pressed against his bare arm.

"Most of your wounds were superficial," she said. "I'm just going to bandage two or three."

He turned his head a little to speak, but that brought their mouths within an inch of each other and he forgot what he'd been about to say.

She ran her fingers down his cheek. "Hmm, soft," she purred. "I like you all clean shaven."

That was it, that was enough. He moved the fraction of an inch it took to claim her lips, reaching around to clasp her shoulder and urge her around and into his lap.

She came with a sweet thud that made his nerve endings skitter like beads of cold water on a hot rock. His hands traveled up and down her supple body as his tongue teased apart her lips. Her warm weight melting into his lap drove him mad; the wet, hot touch of her tongue entwined with his sent flames shooting through his groin.

He inched his hands under her shirt, her skin so soft it rivaled satin. He kissed her with the longing of lost love and maybe something else, maybe with hope. He cupped her breasts and licked the lace cups of her bra, her moans echoing inside his head.

"Simon, Simon, time," she mumbled, and he reluctantly opened his eyes. Hers were open, too. They were deep, deep blue, her lips as she whispered reminding him of rose petals. "We don't have time," she whispered.

Time? What did time have to do with anything? *Everything*....

He'd lost his head.

He swallowed the boulder in his throat and gripped her arms, leaning his forehead against her chest, the incredibly soft, rounded tips of her breasts cushioning his chin. They sat crumpled together for the minute or two it took for their heartbeats to slow, their hormones to recede. Every part of his body throbbed with either desire or pain. The truth was, there wasn't a heck of a lot of difference between the two.

She finally cupped his cheeks and raised his face to hers. He could tell she wanted to say something and was weighing if she should or not. Feeling he'd probably done enough to confuse her already, he was silent, but now that she'd mentioned time, it occurred to him they'd better get on the road again.

"A few hours ago you tried to convince me you'd fallen for me," she said at last.

He nodded but his mind was chasing its own tail in his head. He felt as though he'd been lying to her since the moment he found her in Rocky Point—would she ever forgive him and had the past few minutes just made things worse? He trailed a finger down her long throat. Knowing who and what she was when her memory was intact, he realized the answer was a resounding no. She would be furious he'd kept things from her.

And face it, she had one giant thing, or rather, one tiny being, she could keep from him if she chose. He glanced down at her stomach and then away. She could disappear as she apparently had in the past, and he would never know where she had gone.

"Well," he said, attempting to lighten things up, "I think I just proved it, don't you?"

"It seemed kind of mutual to me," she said, kissing his ear, her breath warm and sweet as it tickled his newly shaved skin. "After we meet with my father, after we find out what he wants, after we go back to Blue Mountain, do you think there's a chance for us?"

"There's always a chance," he said, alarmed at how her words touched his heart. Had he always hoped she would come around? He wasn't sure anymore. And what about her baby? How long could he keep a secret from her that involved her own body?

Unless she already knew and thought she was keeping it from him.

"Don't look so trapped," she whispered.

"I—"

"I know I'm not a mermaid," she said.

"No, you're not," he told her honestly. "No, you're real flesh and blood, all right."

"Damn straight." Their eyes met again. "It's getting late," she added. "Let me fix your bandages, and then we'd better get going."

With an assist from him, she got to her feet, gaze averted. She applied the ointments and gauze with haste, her touch almost impersonal. He finished dressing as she took a quick shower. When she came back into the room a few minutes later, she was dressed in her jeans and the blue sweatshirt. Her short dark hair curled enticingly around her face.

It struck him with a jolt she'd never been a natural blonde, that she'd been bleaching her hair. This new color wasn't a disguise; it was done to make her look more the way she used to when these old men apparently either knew her or had a photograph of her. The long blond hair had been the disguise. Judging from the hack job, he wondered if Carl had cut it himself.

He should tell her about Robert Connors knifed in the restaurant parking lot. He should tell her how Chopper had looked at the man in the bus depot with absolute loathing…

He should warn her.

If the police failed to act in time, they could meet up with Carl and Chopper again.

But she knew that. They both knew it. She had to go forward, and because she had to, he had to.

Their eyes met and they both looked away. Half-truths lay between them like buried embers, daring the wary to step carefully.

Five minutes later, they were back in the truck, headed for Thunder Lodge and the last contact before finally meeting Ella's father.

UNFORTUNATELY, THE ONLY WAY to get to Thunder Lodge was to travel through the very small town of Storm Creek. Simon drove as quickly as the law allowed while Ella kept her head down. Her heart hammered against her ribs as she considered the possibilities that lay ahead.

One, Chopper and Carl could be here; they could be waiting to follow, madder than ever now because the Red Barn restaurant didn't exist.

Two, the police could have responded to Simon's anonymous call, arrested Chopper and Carl as early as last night if they drove straight through, and Carl could have told them exactly how much Ella was involved. There was the very real possibility that she could be arrested for murder.

Three, Chopper and Carl could have been waylaid by the law or by Jack and they could arrive at the lodge to find her father waiting with open arms. To hell with the open arms, she'd settle for an explanation. Was her father aware of how murderous his plan to reconnect with her was going to be or had it all snowballed at him the same way it had at everyone else?

Which would mean she would see her dad. She was alternately hopeful that seeing him would unleash all her memories and terrified it would open no doors whatsoever and he would be as big a stranger as everyone else.

She snuck an under-the-eyelash glance at Simon and amended that thought. Simon wasn't a stranger. Simon wasn't a dream or a threat or a snippet of memory. He was real and the thought of being in his arms, of feeling his lips on hers made her tremble inside.

She wanted more.

"Stop," she said suddenly.

Simon pulled the truck to the side of the road. "What is it? Did you see someone we know?"

She looked at him, careful to keep her face turned from the street. "No. I…I changed my mind. I don't want to go through with it. What do I need a father for?"

He stared into her eyes and nodded. "Okay."

She grabbed his arm as he lowered his hand to change gears. "No, wait."

He sat there and waited, didn't even check the dash clock or his watch to remind her they were running out of time. She finally said, "Didn't you expect I'd have my memory back by the time we got to this point in our journey?"

He thought for a second before slowly nodding. Wearing his black T-shirt with his dark hair combed away from his forehead, he looked like a man who could take care of anything. Even the scratches and cuts from the day before added a note of toughness to his face that she found reassuring. Simon Task wasn't an easy man to stop.

"Who is my father accused of killing?"

"A man in Chicago and his twenty-year-old son."

"Why would he have killed them?"

Simon looked as though he was going to avoid her question, but then to her surprise, he took her hand. "They got in his way. Listen, Ella, your dad was a cop, which might explain your aversion to law enforcement. He was involved in a huge loan-sharking deal with a street gang. He worked as a collection agent for them, him and another cop who was killed in the arrest. Your father made bail and skipped. He took over five million stolen dollars with him."

"And left me alone with my mother," she said softly.

He sat very still as though sensing she needed time to assimilate this discovery. Finally he sighed. "Okay, for the record, I think you're wise to pack in this thing. We can either surrender to the cops or to a lawyer—"

"No, that's okay," she said, resolve once again coursing through her veins. "Let's go."

"But I thought—"

"I just got cold feet, that's all. I want to know what happened. I *have* to know what happened."

She could tell he wanted to argue, but when he finally glanced at the clock and saw the time, he pulled back onto the street without further comment. She rested a hand on her abdomen and imagined a flutter beneath her fingers. It was almost over. She wanted—she needed— her life back.

They left town without seeing anyone they knew. There was no police presence, either, and Simon mused aloud that the small town might not even have its own department. But a bomb in a public building constituted an act of terrorism, he added, and that meant the feds would be looking for Carl Baxter, too. If they were undercover, they were doing a darn good job of it.

"Did I mention Thunder Lodge is closed until June?" Ella asked. "It's only May. How are we going to get into the lodge?"

"We'll cross that bridge in two miles," Simon said, nodding toward a road sign.

The trees crowded the road, shadowing it from the sun. Every once in a while there would be a spot where the trees thinned and they could see a river meandering through the forest. Ella's heart started pounding with nerves again, her stomach rolling.

"There's the turn," she said, pointing ahead, straining against the seat belt now, anxious to get this over with.

An iron gate stood ajar and they drove through. The road began a gradual incline, the pavement littered with pine needles and winter deadfall. Occasional shafts of sunlight revealed vague traces of tire imprints.

The truck rolled over a wooden bridge. The river running under it was dark blue and clear, dappled with sun that made its way through the lacy canopy of deciduous trees overhead. Birch, Ella decided, their white bark lovely against pale green leaves. As they rambled up the slope on the other side, the tree cover grew less rampant until they emerged into an open field.

The area seemed to be part of a natural meadow, surrounded by towering trees, but relatively flat. Several imposing log buildings ringed the area. There were no other vehicles and no sign of anyone else.

Simon stopped the truck in front of the largest structure and they both got out. As it was the only one without boards shuttering the windows, they gravitated to its wide stone stairs and wooden deck.

Ella gripped the metal handles on the big plank

doors and tugged, but they were securely locked. "Are we that late?" she cried. To have come so far and be left with nothing was more than she could bear.

Simon checked his watch. "Five minutes is all. Remember, the gate was open. Let's look around the other buildings."

Before they could turn, Ella sensed a presence behind them. Something poked her in the back, something that felt an awful lot like a gun barrel.

A male voice demanded, "Let's get those hands up where I can see 'em, folks. Nice and easy, and no one gets hurt."

She looked at Simon.

They both raised their arms.

Chapter Thirteen

Simon didn't recognize the voice, but that didn't come as much of a surprise. He was pretty sure neither Chopper nor Carl Baxter would have been so polite.

He knew what was coming next. Sure enough, whoever was back there slipped Simon's revolver from his waistband holster.

"You can turn around now," the man said.

They both turned.

The weapon turned out to be a Winchester repeating rifle in mint condition, the wooden stock gleaming with polish. The weathered man holding it appeared to be in his late sixties, of average height and weight, his skin deeply grooved. He wore scuffed boots, baggy jeans and a padded blue jacket with a patch or two. The threadbare edges of his quilted cap revealed wisps of longish gray hair.

He might look like a bum, but there was nothing remotely slack in the keen look of the old guy's eyes or in the way he shouldered the rifle. He looked from Simon to Ella, his gaze lingering on her face. Simon, who had assumed they'd run into a cagey caretaker, reassessed his conclusion.

"You haven't changed much since you were a girl," the man said, lowering his weapon.

"I'm sorry," Ella said. "If I ever knew you, I've forgotten."

His brow furrowed and his eyes narrowed. "Do I look that different?"

"I don't know. I was in a car accident a week ago. I've lost my memory. For a while, anyway."

Now his mouth seemed to drop open. "You have amnesia?"

She nodded.

"And yet you came all this way?"

"My father needs me, right?"

"He wants to see you, that's for sure." He glanced up at Simon and added in a censoring tone, "You her husband, what's his name, Carl Baxter?"

"Absolutely not," Simon said.

"My husband is one of the men after me. This man is named Simon Task. I wouldn't have made it this far without his help. It's been very—violent."

"I know about the violence," the old man said. "Jerry and Robert are both dead. I had to read it the newspaper. You know anything about that?"

"Those were the first two contacts," Simon said.

Ella sucked in a breath. "Both of them? The man from the restaurant, too?"

The old guy nodded. "I haven't heard from Potter, either."

"Potter the contact at the bus depot?" Simon said, remembering how Chopper all but spit out his name.

"Yeah. He was supposed to call. He didn't."

"I saw him leave the station," Simon said. "We both did. But like Ella said, there are two armed and dangerous men following us. We've done our best to lose them, but—"

"Well, they aren't following you now. I've got someone on the gate." He reached in his pocket and withdrew a two-way radio. After fooling with the volume, he clicked a button that suspended the static and barked, "You there?"

The reply was equally terse. "Yeah, I'm here."

"You see anyone?"

"Nothing. Neither did Johnny. It's clear. I'm locking the gate. Good luck."

The older man pocketed the radio, then stuck out a hand toward Ella, who shook it. "My name is Reed. I'll take you to your father."

"But aren't you frightened?" Ella said. "The other men—"

"It's got to be done," he interrupted, "and trust me, if those fellows were still on your trail, Merle and Johnny would know about it." He looked down at her feet and added, "Good, you have decent shoes. Do you have a coat?"

"In the truck."

"Get it. My Jeep is around back. We'll drive a ways, but then we'll have to go the rest of the way on foot."

Simon stepped forward. "I'm coming with you."

"No, you're not."

Wondering if Ella would back him up, he said, "Then she doesn't go."

Reed glanced at Ella. "Is that your position?"

Much to Simon's relief, she nodded.

Reed narrowed his eyes as he studied Simon, finally saying, "You're a damn cop or military, something like that."

"Yes."

"You out to capture her father?"

"No. He's in no danger from me."

"Okay, you can come. Lock your truck. Come on, we've got a long way to go to reach camp."

As Ella and Simon gathered their coats and a few belongings from the truck, Reed disappeared around back, reappearing a few minutes later in a battered old Jeep. The rifle lay on the passenger floor, the passenger seat stacked with sleeping bags and backpacks.

Simon and Ella climbed into the back. Simon said, "How about returning my gun?"

"Later. Hold on now, it's a bit of a bumpy ride."

Simon exchanged a long glance with Ella. She'd pulled on the knit cap and looked like a kid on her first camping trip. Traces of her facial wounds were faint now, and in the afternoon light, her blue eyes sparkled more than the river. She was either excited to be out in nature or anxious to see her father, or maybe both.

They stopped after a couple of miles when the road came to an abrupt end. Climbing out of the old Jeep, they found themselves across a broad chasm from a waterfall that fell in a sheet of silver, pouring over the lip high above, falling into a pool before rushing down the river toward the lodge. The sides of the chasm were lush with vegetation, splashes of color thanks to wildflowers making it look like a secret garden. It was gorgeous and, at any other time, Simon would have itched to wander the isolated paths with Ella at his side.

Reed handed Simon his revolver. "Grab a pack," he added as Simon fit the gun back into its holster. "I only brought two but there's plenty of food."

"You're not leaving your truck here, are you?" Simon added.

"Where else would I leave it?"

"Someplace where it doesn't point a giant finger at us saying 'They went that away.'"

"I told you, no one came through the gate

after you. Anyway, it's not my Jeep. Merle will get it later."

"Merle will just have to hunt for it, then. You don't know these two thugs who are following us." Simon stretched out his hand. "Give me the keys. I saw a big clump of trees and an old building half a mile back. I'll tuck it back in there. You two sweep the area, cover up the tracks in the clearing, I'll catch up."

Reed tossed Simon the Jeep key, shaking his head as he did so. Simon drove the truck back down the road and parked it out of sight. Dragging a branch behind him, he obscured the tracks on his way back to the clearing.

As soon as Reed saw Simon return, he shouldered his pack. Ella was leaning over a small white flower. "Trillium," she said as she stood. "I tried to grow some once."

Just like that, she'd gained another insight. She grinned. "I have a garden. I have a house. Gray with white shutters and a red front door. If only I could remember who used to walk through the door. Maybe my father."

"Maybe," Simon said. It wouldn't be long before she realized *he'd* walked through her front door a hundred times.

"Time's a-passing, folks," Reed said.

Despite Ella's insistence she be the one to carry

the backpack, Simon got to it first. He took a deep breath as it settled against his back.

Reed took the lead and for an old guy he was no slouch. Simon brought up the rear. The path was easy going for a while, meandering its way up the mountain, away from the waterfall, and then back to it. But it was soon obvious the path was more or less abandoned. There were whole sections where the wooden supports for the stepped slope had rotted away, leaving it to each of them to find footing, holding on to branches and each other at times to keep from slipping.

Simon glanced behind them as much as he did forward. It was hard to picture Chopper or Carl climbing a mountain, but not impossible. He also did his best to put a lid on his growing annoyance with the whole situation. What in the hell was going on? Hiking? Her father couldn't just show up at the lodge like a regular guy? How many hoops were they going to have to jump through? He hurried past Ella, who had stopped to admire a patch of small purple flowers, catching up to Reed.

"I assume we're crossing into Canada," he said.

Reed spared him a quick glance. "We might."

"And judging from the sleeping bags and other equipment, we're out here for at least one night."

"Nothing gets past you," Reed growled. Simon was kind of glad to hear the strained quality of the older man's breathing. He'd hate to think a man pushing seventy had more stamina than he did.

"So what's in it for you?" Simon persisted.

Reed stopped walking and turned to face him. He took off his ratty hat, wiped his brow with his sleeve and gestured down the trail. "If your job is to watch out for her, maybe you ought to go tear her away from those flowers. We're losing daylight." And with that, he pulled on his hat and resumed climbing.

Simon swore under his breath as he watched Reed scramble uphill. He looked back for Ella, but she was already walking toward him.

Another hour put them near a small pool. Looking up the hillside, Simon could see the top of the falls disappearing into thickening cloud cover. The lush vegetation served as a reminder that spring was damp this far north. He found himself hoping Thunder Lodge got its name because of some old legend and not because of the weather.

The sound of the falls meant Reed had to raise his voice to be heard. "This is as far as we go tonight. Can't take a chance on falling. I remembered this spot being larger, but it's been years since I was here last and I didn't remember the trail being so bad, either. An old man's memory, you know."

Simon allowed the pack to drop to the ground, happy to stop. It had been torture having that heavy thing bounce against his back as he walked. He was either sweaty or bloody under his shirt and the truth was he didn't really want to know which.

As Ella unrolled their sleeping bag a few feet away, Reed started gathering fallen wood. Simon hitched his hands on his waist. "What are you doing?" he demanded. "You're not thinking of starting a fire, are you?"

"Sure, why not? It'll get cold soon."

"A fire will act as a beacon," Simon said.

Reed chuckled as he snapped a long branch in half across his knee. "Mr. Task, please. From Thunder Lodge, there's one way to go on this mountain and that's up. They don't need to see a fire to find us if they're back there, which I sincerely doubt. Besides, take a look around you. If we build it near the cliff wall, it'll be invisible from down below until you practically stumble into it."

Simon did just that—he looked around. Reed had a point, and one glance at Ella's wilted form and wan complexion sealed the deal. "Just make it a small one," he said.

"Sure."

Simon shook his head, but in the end, he took over fire duties while Reed produced a few freeze-dried foil-wrapped packets. As the last of the daylight fled, they sat around the small blaze eating reconstituted beef Stroganoff and drinking tea made from boiled water. Simon felt as though there were a target painted on his forehead and another on his back as he sat in the flickering light of the small blaze.

"How much farther do we hike tomorrow?" he asked Reed. Ella had moved close to the fire, her knees drawn up to her chest, her arms looped around her legs. She'd been gazing into the fire, but at the sound of Simon's voice, she looked up. Firelight played with her features as she stared at Reed, waiting for an answer.

"Less you know, the better," Reed said.

"I don't agree," Simon insisted. "How can I be prepared if I don't know what's going on?"

"That's what I'm here for."

"We don't even know who you are," Simon protested.

"I'm Reed. I'm the next link in her crazy father's crazy chain. That's all you need to know."

"Yeah, well, sorry for bringing this up, but our contacts don't seem to last long once they talk to us."

Reed dismissed this concern with a gesture of his hand. "I'm the most careful of the bunch." He produced a packet of cigarettes and shook one free. "Anyone mind if I smoke?"

"Yes," Ella and Simon said in unison.

He glowered at them. As he flicked the unlit cigarette into the fire, Simon pressed on. "Let's say you have a heart attack tonight," he said pleasantly. "Or maybe a bear eats you. How do we proceed?"

"Keep going up the trail to the top of the falls."

"And my father will be there?" Ella asked.

"Sooner or later. Stop worrying."

"Stop worrying?" Ella snapped. She sat up straighter. "Do you have any idea how many times I've almost died in the past week? And how about Simon? I believe we have more than a little right to be worried."

Reed studied her for a second before speaking, his expression difficult to read. "Okay, okay, all I meant is we'll keep the fire lit so the bears stay away." He smiled and added, "And there's nothing wrong with my damn heart."

"You smoke. That's hard on a heart," she grumbled.

"Just one after dinner," Reed said.

"Why this complicated and deadly system for a man to talk to his daughter?" she persisted.

"He's a wanted murderer. Some people want the cash he took, some want him held accountable for his actions."

"Did he really kill that man and his son?"

Reed stared at her a second before nodding.

"And now he's set in motion a plan that's getting more people killed."

"No one anticipated all the death."

"Do you know the two men who are after us?" Simon asked. "Carl Baxter and a guy called Chopper?"

Reed's bushy eyebrows knit together over his pale eyes. "I meant to ask about that, Ella. Your own husband is threatening you?"

"Ex-husband," she insisted, but ruined her authority by glancing at Simon and mumbling, "At least I hope so."

Things fell silent for a few moments as the fire crackled. All of a sudden, Ella said, "I remember a man saying he recognized someone named Potter. It's like it happened in a dream, though. Wait, it was in the car after they drugged me. That's where I heard it."

"It must have been Chopper," Simon said as he pictured the moment Potter and Chopper had locked gazes at the bus station. A sizzle of recognition had charged the air. He'd seen it. He'd *felt* it, he'd even mentioned it to Ella and then he'd forgotten all about it. "I saw them meet. They knew each other."

"Who are you talking about?" Reed demanded.

"The other man. We just know him as Chopper."

"Chopper," Reed mused. "I don't know—"

"Big guy," Simon added. "Dark clothes and complexion."

"Very fond of his knife," Ella added.

Reed looked at her quickly. "What kind of knife?"

"A long curved blade. Mean looking."

"A kukri?"

"I'm not familiar—"

Reed quickly grabbed a stick from the pile of collected firewood and sketched a knife in the loose dirt. "Like this?"

They both leaned forward to look. He'd drawn a knife about ten inches long with a curved blade. "Yes. Very much like that," Ella said.

"It's British army standard issue for the Gurkhas Unit."

"The what?"

Reed shook his head as he scuffed out the line drawing he'd made in the dirt with his boot and threw the stick in the fire.

"The Gurkhas are a military unit composed of men from northern India and Nepal," Simon said. Narrowing his eyes, he added, "So, Reed, why does the mention of the kukri make you look like you saw a ghost?"

Reed got to his feet so abruptly he stumbled and reached out for a fallen log to brace himself. "I'll take first watch," he said. "Get some sleep."

"You're not going to explain, are you?" Simon persevered. "Why? You know, I looked up Ella's father on the Internet. I know what he did, I know why he ran."

"So many years ago," Reed mumbled. "Anyway, it's impossible."

"What's impossible? And sixteen years is not that long. I think you and the cops who have been acting as contacts must have all been still working together in Chicago—"

"I will not discuss this," Reed snapped, leveling a stare that announced question-and-answer period was over. "Flashlights in my pack, each of you take one." He shouldered his rifle and stalked out of their tiny camp, choosing a rock at the far end of the pool on which to perch, just out of the light cast by the fire.

Simon tore his attention from Reed's hasty exit to find that Ella had begun cleaning up the garbage from dinner. He joined her in sealing the used packets, cups and silverware in plastic so the refuse wouldn't attract wild animals, stowing it away to pack out with them the next morning. They went about their work silently, banking the fire, retrieving the flashlights from Reed's pack. There wasn't a whole lot to say, although Simon's mind raced. Who was Chopper? Potter had recognized him and so had Reed, or at least he'd recognized the knife.

"I have to visit the little girl's room out in the trees," Ella said, an urgent tone to her voice.

"I'll stand guard."

"No, that's okay, I'm fine," she said, and quickly grabbed her flashlight and disappeared into the trees, but he'd seen her hand fly up to cover her mouth. Morning sickness seemed to have been replaced by evening sickness.

Eventually, they both prepared for bed and lay down next to each other in the ample sleeping bag. There was only room to lay on their sides spoon fashion, and since his back was the one resembling hamburger, he took the outside position. This meant she was curled close to him, her back to his front.

"What are you thinking about?" he asked her when he found he couldn't get to sleep.

She turned her head to speak to him. Her breath smelled like peppermint. "I was thinking I wished Reed would go far away so you and I could finish what we started earlier."

He smiled into the dark. "Sounds nice."

"Nice? Is that all?"

"No, that's not all," he said, and inched closer. He licked her earlobe, something that had once driven her crazy, and by the way her hips moved, he was pretty sure it still did. In deference to their current situation, he limited himself to nuzzling her neck.

"Do you miss her?" Ella whispered.

"Miss who?"

"The mermaid. Do you wish she were here with you?"

"I don't want anyone here right now but you," he hedged, and once again chided himself. Something was going to trigger her memory. Something would bring it all back and he wanted her to understand where he'd been coming from, but that wasn't going to happen if he didn't find a way to level with her.

Keep telling yourself you don't care about her, his subconscious whispered.

"Me, either," she said.

"Good."

"Tell me what a Saturday is like for you," she said around a yawn.

"You mean when I'm not working?"

"Yeah. Just an ordinary Saturday. What do you eat for breakfast?"

As he described fresh bagels bought at a bakery in downtown Blue Mountain, she snuggled against his chest. The top of her head was cool against his arm, her hair redolent of campfire smoke.

"Then I work on an old BMW my dad and I are rebuilding together," he added. "I used to listen to the radio while I worked, to a gardening show my friend does. Sometimes her show is about cooking. She changes it up week to week. I just liked hearing her voice."

"That sounds nice," Ella whispered, her warm breath tickling the inside of his arm. "What next?"

"Let's see. Dinner, I guess. Sometimes I go out and sometimes my friend invites me over. Well, she used to. She's a wonderful cook. Her specialty is seafood. What she can do with scallops is enough to make a man cry."

Ella snuggled closer. Her bottom was against his groin and it was work not letting it get to him. "You're talking about the mermaid, aren't you?" she whispered.

"Yes."

"You're making me hungry."

She was making him hungry, too, but not for food. He stroked her hair, ran a hand down her arm.

As wonderful as it was to hold her, it was also deceitful. She had no idea of what she used to mean to him, what she still meant to him. Had he kind of hoped mentioning her voice on the radio and her scallops Provençal would tweak a memory? Yes, of course. After several minutes of arguing with himself over the right thing to do, he spoke.

"I have something to tell you," he whispered, stretching his fingers to brush the curve of her abdomen.

It seemed to him she stopped breathing. Before she could start asking questions, he continued. "I haven't been sure how much to tell you. Well, I admitted that once, didn't I? I told you my cousin, the doctor, suggested I play it safe and let you remember what you could when you could? And then so much has been going on, but the truth is I was also kind of afraid. I let you believe things— well, hell, okay, I lied. Anyway, here's the truth. Yes, you and I knew each other before you lost your memory. Back in Blue Mountain. We were lovers. Things started going wrong a couple of weeks ago. We had a fight. Oh, hell, the truth is I stormed out."

Her silence was deafening. On the other hand, she hadn't pulled away, so maybe there was hope. "Ella?" he whispered. "Say something. Ask anything you want."

Still no response. For several seconds he held his breath until it finally dawned on him she was asleep; his confession had gone unheard.

He considered shaking her awake, but in the end, gently kissed the top of her head instead. He'd try again tomorrow—before it was too late. Before he lost her completely.

Chapter Fourteen

Her father stood right in front of her, but when she reached for him, the movement of her hands dissipated his form into a mist that reshaped when she gave up trying to touch him. He had no face but it was him.

She closed her eyes. When she reopened them, she found Carl where her father had been. He was holding a plate and she screamed. The next thing she knew, they were flying. Carl held the plate in front of him, one hand on each rim. She grabbed for it and it shattered into a million pieces.

Tears rolled under her chin and down her blouse, between her breasts, down her belly, a virtual river of tears. She held her hands up and they turned into trees—

She awoke with a jolt.

The weather had changed. Her hair was damp, raindrops sliding down her forehead and cheeks.

Simon knelt beside her, barely visible in the dim light of predawn.

"Are you okay?" he asked.

"I'm…I'm fine," she stammered, blinking rapidly.

"It just started raining," he said. "Let's get our stuff under the trees, okay?"

The trees. She looked over his head at the towering gray silhouettes of the trees, their boughs waving in the wind, their rustling vaguely evocative of the ocean.

"I dreamed about my father," she said.

Simon paused in his task of rolling his damp sleeping bag. "Anything we can use?"

"No, he disappeared as usual. Oh, get this, Carl made a cameo."

Simon's eyebrows raised. As anything to do with Carl was creepy, she quickly added, "Don't worry, he was just driving a plate."

Simon chuckled and kept working.

The rain increased and she pulled her hood up over her hair, hustling now to get her things under some kind of cover. Simon had earmarked a grove of evergreen trees. As they deposited everything in relative dryness, Ella looked around the campsite. It didn't take full daylight to see she and Simon were alone.

"Where is he?" she asked as she perched her rear on a fallen tree.

"Reed?" Simon sat down next to her. "I don't know. He woke me up a few hours ago to take over the watch, then disappeared again."

She hadn't heard Reed summon Simon, nor had she awoken when he extricated himself from the sleeping bag. She must have been out like a zombie. "He's a hard man to figure," she said.

"He turned white when he heard about Chopper's knife."

"True. Aren't you kind of wondering where Chopper and Carl are? It seems too good to be true that Jack managed to stop them for good. For that matter, he said he wasn't even going to try to stop them, just delay them."

"Maybe the police apprehended them," Simon said. "Otherwise I think you could count on them being in this camp right now. Between the campfire and all our noise, this hasn't exactly been a stealth operation."

"If they're in custody, who knows what Carl is telling them? Probably blaming me for killing those two men."

He put an arm around her shoulders. "Let's take things one disaster at a time, okay?"

"I hope they didn't hurt Jack," she said.

"He seemed like the kind of man who can take care of himself," Simon said.

She could see the gray of his eyes now. His beard had started to grow again, defining the strong curve of his jaw. He added, "You're shaking. Are you nervous? Today's the big day."

"Hell yes, I'm nervous. It's not every day a person gets to meet her estranged father. But I'm shaking because I'm cold."

"I have a spare sweatshirt stuffed into my pack. Want it?"

"Absolutely."

While she took off her jacket, he dug in the pack, finally pulling out a university sweatshirt she hadn't seen him wear. At the same time, a sock came flying out of the pack and landed by her foot with a thud.

She instinctively reached for it, aware that Simon had, too. Her fingers closed on the soft cotton first, but it was obvious something roundish and heavy was stuffed into the toe of the sock. She lifted it and handed it to him, eyebrows raised.

He shrugged.

She pulled the sweatshirt over her head. What was he hiding?

By the time she popped her head out of the shirt and pushed her arms into the sleeves, he'd peeled away the sock. He held a small globe in his hand. Encased within the globe was an otter swimming on its back, a clamshell on its tummy. Silver glitter fell through the trapped glycerin like sparkling raindrops.

Zipping her jacket over the sweatshirt, she said, "What's that?"

"A memento," he said, and handed it to her.

She took it, her gaze fastened to his gray eyes. Looking down at the globe, she said, "It's cute."

"Would you like it?" he asked.

A smile tugged at her lips. "Yes."

"It's yours," he said, closing her fingers around the plastic dome.

A noise in the trees sent both of them to their feet. A moment later, Reed emerged from the underbrush. Ella slipped the globe into her pocket. She liked the way she could feel it resting against her leg.

"Where have you been?" Simon asked as his gun went back in the holster.

Reed held up a creel. In his other hand, he held a compact fishing rod. "Been catching breakfast. Anyone like trout?"

This time they found a rocky overhang under which to start a small fire. Reed produced a frying pan and with little fanfare fried three rainbow trout to perfection. They took turns eating the fish right from the pan. It took almost an hour to be ready to go again, but Ella had to admit the warm food sat better in her stomach than anything had in several days. Maybe she was getting over the incessant nausea. Happy thought.

But about the only one.

The nightly dreams featuring her father were growing increasingly bizarre and unfulfilling, and meeting Reed hadn't helped foster any warm, fuzzy scenarios. She fingered the globe in her pocket as she thought about the man she was soon to meet.

He'd taken huge amounts of money and apparently still wielded enough power to engage men like Reed and the others to do what he told them to do despite the danger. He had to be a cold, heartless man and Ella couldn't help wondering if she'd kept in close contact with him over the years or if she hadn't seen him since he ran away. She must have been twelve at the time. And he'd left her with an abusive mother, she was pretty sure about that.

This time, she got to the pack first and had it adjusted on her back before Simon could protest. They adopted the same formation as the day before, Reed in front, Simon bringing up the rear. This far up the mountain, the trail was more of a suggestion than an actual path. The waterfall was on their right as they ascended, though they lost sight of it on occasion. They climbed in silence, each caught up in the chore of just getting a little farther along.

An hour went by, then two. It wasn't until Ella stopped to take a deep breath and turned her face up to the sky in order to stretch her aching back that she realized the rain had stopped. The spring sunlight felt like a heat lamp.

Simon caught up with her. As he brushed a curl from her forehead he gazed at her with troubled gray eyes. "I want you to stay near me," he said as they resumed walking, this time more or less together. "Behind me, if you can. We don't know what to expect, so expect anything and everything."

He was talking about possible danger. He was talking about flying bullets and abductions and knives. The enormity of what she was possibly subjecting someone else to really hit home.

Her hand fluttered against her abdomen as she took a half-dozen steps and then she stopped and turned to look at him. "There's something you have to know."

"Okay. Go ahead. What?"

"I think I'm pregnant."

His gaze remained steady. The man was truly unflappable. She added, "I wanted you to know because it means there might be two of me to protect."

"How long have you suspected?" he asked.

"Since after the abduction, after the first time we went to the library. That's why I haven't had time or opportunity to buy a test."

She was sure she saw the gears spinning and turning in back of his eyes, but he didn't say anything.

"Okay," she finished lamely. "Well, now you know."

"Now I know. It explains a lot."

"I wish it explained who the father was." *Please, not Carl...*

"You'll know soon," Simon said. "We'd better catch up with Reed. We're almost at the top."

She nodded and turned, but he caught her arm and she looked back over her shoulder at him.

"You're going to make a great mother, Ella."

"Do you think so?"

"I really do. And I'll be there for you if you'll let me."

"Why wouldn't I let you?"

"Oh, you know, things happen and—"A sound up ahead cut off his words. "Falling rock," he murmured as he drew his weapon and stepped in front of her. "Reed?" he yelled.

The path twisted and turned as it climbed and though Ella peered ahead, she could see no sign of the older man. At last they heard his voice. "I'm okay, I'm okay. Just a little stumble."

Over his shoulder, Simon said, "Let me go ahead."

She nodded, falling into step a second behind him. Around the second bend, they came across Reed sitting on the ground, holding his ankle, swearing. From the look of things, he'd lost his footing on a patch of small rocks.

Simon reholstered his revolver as Ella knelt beside Reed. "Is anything broken?"

"No, just twisted or sprained. I'm okay," Reed said. He grabbed hold of a bigger rock and used it to push himself to his feet, glaring at Ella when she reached out to steady him.

"I'm fine," he insisted.

"Maybe we should take off your boot."

"No," Simon said. "Better keep it on in case his foot starts to swell. We can't have much farther to go."

"Not far," Reed agreed. He shrugged his arm away from Ella and started walking again. Ella and Simon exchanged glances when they saw his limp, but they fell dutifully in line behind him.

Eventually, Ella spied a red dot off to the west and pointed it out to the men. Shading her eyes and peering into the distant sky, she could barely discern the dragonfly shape of an approaching helicopter.

"My father?" Ella whispered, trembling inside. It was almost over. Her memory would come back—she would know who she was, she could go back to her life, she could nourish a new life—heck, she could know who to inform he was going to be a father. Her fingers danced over the globe in her pocket.

"He's early," Reed grumbled.

"Maybe he's just anxious to see his daughter," Simon said.

"Of course he is," Reed agreed, and once again continued walking, the limp growing more pronounced with each step. "There's a gullylike thing we have to navigate up ahead, and then we're there," he added.

The gully turned out to be a narrow, rocky chute, deeply channeled and uneven. Reed stopped to lean against an exposed root of a towering pine. His foot obviously hurt him. The waterfall was very close at this point on the trail and it was too noisy to converse.

Simon tapped his chest and stepped ahead of Reed. He negotiated the tricky footing by climbing onto a boulder-size rock, then more or less sliding down the other side. Ella followed. As Simon gained ground, he reached out for Ella to help her. She, in turn, reached back for Reed, but he hadn't followed and gestured for her to go on.

At last Simon hauled her up the last precarious few feet, where they erupted onto the wide riverbed. The river itself was dark and swift, cascading over the lip, fed by the spring runoff from the Canadian Rockies. Huge flat rocks jutted up at random intervals. The forest crowded the edges of the bed. The ground beside the river was muddy, slippery.

Ella spared a quick look down the waterfall as Simon paused, she supposed to wait for Reed. It had to be a four-hundred-foot drop, a cascade of torrential water intent on fulfilling its destiny.

Simon tugged on her arm, pointed at himself and then back down the chute. She nodded her understanding and watched as he disappeared back the way they'd come. She shook her head— she knew Reed would hate taking help from Simon almost as much as he hated taking help from her. He wasn't the kind of guy who asked for or accepted a lending hand with grace.

She took a deep breath and perched atop a rock, searching the sky for the helicopter, which she'd lost sight of during the past several minutes. It cleared the trees about a half mile away and began a descent toward her.

Though Ella was sweaty from the climb, she broke into chills as the pilot chose a solid-looking spot of smaller rocks set back from the water about a quarter of a mile away. The blades sent sand and grit into a swirling cloud as it hovered.

Merging worlds spun in her head. Her past and her future raced toward each other. Too late now to stop even if she wanted to. She got to her feet and began walking over the uneven rocks, breaking into a trot, her heart lodged in her throat as the copter touched down.

As the propellers spun to a halt, she shrugged the pack off her back and let it fall to the rocky ground. Bracing her hands on her knees, she took deep breaths.

This was it. The moment she'd been waiting for was upon her.

The pilot's door opened as she straightened up. An older man climbed out. He stood tall and straight, a leather bomber jacket worn with panache. The smile of greeting she'd felt flowering on her lips wilted and died as he pinned her in place with bright blue eyes.

She squinted against the glare off the helicopter, trying to see the man's features, trying to record them, recall them. He looked exactly as Ella had imagined he would, from the high forehead to the straight silver hair. Tyler Starling, her father, looked enough like her that she knew it would set every Starling bone in her body humming with recognition.

This was it.

Simon pulled Reed up the last few feet of the chute. The old man glowered at him. Well, what had he expected? They hadn't exactly been buddy-buddy during this trek; no reason for that to change now.

Once at the top, they both looked around at the impressive scenery, but Simon suspected Reed was also looking for Ella, just as he was.

They both spotted the bright red helicopter at the same time. It looked like a Bell JetRanger to Simon. Ella stood near it, facing a man wearing a brown jacket. The two of them reminded him of the acrylic snow globe Ella now carried in her pocket. Two figures facing each other, frozen in time instead of plastic.

"Damn," Simon muttered. "I shouldn't have left her up here alone."

"No one asked you to come back for me," Reed said as he dropped the pack from his back and leaned it against a rock. "I would have made it okay."

Simon ignored him and started walking. The old man limped but kept pace, navigating the uneven ground pretty well, all things considered. "Did her father come alone?" Simon asked.

"That was the plan."

"I can't see past the glare on the windshield. There could be someone else in the chopper. Let's go faster." Simon could think of nothing to do but get to Ella's side as soon as possible. There was no covert way to approach and rushing in like a storm trooper would be counterproductive at best. "If I'm right, that machine has about a three-hundred-mile range," he said as they walked. "Did her dad come from three hundred miles away or is he going to travel that far when he leaves here?"

"The airport isn't far. We're not as remote as it may seem. Things have become…uncomfortable…in Canada. He's leaving."

"Why a copter?"

Reed shrugged again. "Why not? The man is rich, he's on the run, not a bad way to get around, right?"

"I guess." He kept his opinion to himself, but a wanted murderer living the high life rubbed him the wrong way. He was surprised it didn't rub Reed the wrong way, too. His suspicions were right, Reed had once been a cop like the first two contacts. He'd known her father, or at least it sure sounded as though he had and maybe still did. According to the brief newspaper report he'd seen, Tyler Starling's actions had shamed the whole Chicago police department.

They were close enough now for Simon to see the face of the man by the helicopter. While he'd not really stopped to think about what Tyler Starling would look like, this guy was perfect. But no one seemed to be talking. As Simon crossed the last few feet to Ella's side, he tried to get a clear view inside, but the reflection on the bubble still obliterated everything.

Halting behind her, he touched her elbow. "Ella?" He met her father's impersonal gaze and tried a nod. "Ella, let's all walk away from the helicopter, okay?" With a glance, he included Ella's dad in the invitation.

Ella shook her head as she turned to look up at him. "I have a million images in my head," she said. "They're all disjointed. You, my house, thousands of trees for some dumb reason, my mother's face, my father disappearing into thin air—they're all inside my head but it doesn't make sense. Seeing my father has done nothing to jog my memory."

"Give it a bit."

Ella's dad remained statue still. Ella took a few steps toward him. "Dad?" she said.

Starling's expression didn't change. It was as though his emotions had been spent years before. Why didn't he speak? Why arrange such a meeting if—

No, wait a second. Starling didn't look indifferent, he looked terrified.

At the same moment Starling reached out to Ella as if to warn her away, Simon sensed movement in the helicopter interior. His hand went for his gun, but before he could draw, the crack of a bullet exploded and Tyler Starling sagged to the ground.

Ella ran to her father, catching his falling form in her arms as Carl Baxter jumped from the copter to the rocks. Simon had his gun out and he was pretty sure Reed had unshouldered the rifle, but Baxter already had his gun pointed at Ella.

Chopper rounded the front of the machine, his big curved knife held at his side, an assault rifle looped over his shoulder. He took one look at the fallen man and screamed. "You shot him, you bastard. He was mine to kill, not yours."

Baxter spared the big man an impatient sneer. "Will you please try to keep your eye on the big picture?"

Chopper sheathed the knife and slung the rifle around in front of him.

Reed whispered, "William Smith and Sanjay Chopra working together? God help us."

Chapter Fifteen

Under her father's sagging weight, Ella folded to the ground, cradling him in her lap. His blood seeped into her clothes, his breathing was irregular and rattled, blood bubbled on his lips. The pressure of a cold circle of steel against the back of her neck was the only sensation her brain registered.

"Once again, I seem to hold all the cards," Carl said, talking over her head. "You two put down your weapons or the little lady gets shot right where she sits."

Vaguely aware of the sound of weapons hitting the rocks, Ella leaned in close to her dad's face. "Can you hear me?" she whispered. "Please, answer me."

His eyes seemed to focus on hers and then he took a shuddering breath. In the next instant, his mouth went slack. With a growing sense of shock, Ella realized her father was dead.

Carl grabbed her arm, pulling so hard she had

no choice but to stumble to her feet as her dad's body slipped to the riverbank. Tears of loss and fury burned behind her nose.

She turned on Carl and, heedless of the gun in his hand, beat on his chest with her fists. "You killed him," she screamed. "You bastard, you killed my father before he could say anything to me. How could you? How could you?" The tears rolled freely now, but she didn't care, she was too devastated to care.

Carl used his gun-free hand to slap her. Even as her neck jerked back, she saw Simon try to help her. For his efforts, Chopper swung the butt of his gun into Simon's mouth. Enraged even more, she went berserk, lashing out at Carl in any way she could until he caught both her shoulders and shook her.

"You silly bitch," he hissed. "You don't know, do you?"

Something in his voice and the smile twisting his lips froze the sobs in her throat.

He spun her around. Simon stood a few feet away, gray eyes blazing, blood dripping down his chin from the gash across his bottom lip. Reed stood next to him, pale to the point of bleached laundry.

"*That's* your father," Carl said, pointing, but not at the dead pilot.

Her gaze met Simon's for one heartbeat. In the next, they both looked at Reed.

"IS IT TRUE?" she finally whispered.

Reed stared at her, his lips drawn into a tight, straight line.

"Ah, come on, Tyler," Carl said. "Tell her all about it."

Ella glanced at the fallen man. "He looks just as I knew he would. Who was *he?*"

"Bob Rydell," Carl said. "Like the other contacts you met, he was a cop with your father back in Chicago when you were a kid. No relation, Eleanor, just a happy coincidence he seemed familiar."

Fixing her stare on Reed or Starling or whoever he was, Ella whispered, "Why?"

He rubbed his jaw. "Why did they risk their lives? Because they owed me. They were fulfilling a debt."

"Not that," Ella murmured. "Why didn't you tell me who you were yesterday?"

Her father studied the rocks, a knot in his jaw.

"Just give me a straight answer," she demanded.

"It wasn't supposed to be like this," he muttered, and for once he didn't sound so sure of himself. "I planned the hike up the mountain so we would have time to talk and get to know each other. I knew your brother had been captured and killed down in Tierra Montañosa. I knew you were alone.

"Anyway, I was leaving today to start over again

somewhere new. This hike was my last chance to explain what happened all those years ago and to give you money, you know, to take care of you. When you got to the lodge and didn't know who I was, when you barely knew who you were, well, I wasn't sure what to do so I just let you assume I was the next contact. I just wanted to buy some time. I put off talking to you. I'm sorry."

"You're a stranger to me," she said.

"I can see that. Ultimate irony, isn't it? I risk all this, three men are dead—"

"Four," the man Reed had called Sanjay Chopra interjected as he stepped closer, the rifle clutched in his white-knuckled hands.

Starling groaned. "You got Cal Potter?"

"How else would we have known about the helicopter?" Chopra's dark eyes gleamed like shards of obsidian as he added, "You murdered my father and brother because they wouldn't go along with your schemes. They were good, decent men. My father was a former Gurkha, a man of strength and honor."

The big man's mouth twisted and his nostrils flared. In one fluid movement, he looped the assault rifle over his shoulder again and released the kukri knife from its scabbard. Holding it balanced on his fingers, he said, "When neither of them would be cowered by the murdering criminals you served, you killed them. Then you stole from the very thieving devils you worked for. You ran like the coward you were, like the coward you will always be."

"You've got this all wrong," Starling said carefully. "I'm not the one who killed your family. I'm the one who took the rap, I'm the one who got the others off free. I was the one who had the least to stick around for, the least to lose, so I'm the one they all paid off.

"So, yes, I'm guilty in some ways for your father's and brother's deaths. If I'd talked up when I first knew about the deep corruption on the force—and it went all the way up to the top—if I'd been as honorable as you say your family was, maybe i wouldn't have happened the way it did." He looked down at the man dead on the rocks and added, "This is the man who pulled the trigger. Him and the others, they're the ones who were involved."

"I will not listen to your lies," Chopra bellowed "I've waited all these years, keeping track of each of the men who helped you escape, knowing sooner or later one of them would lead me to you. And now, thanks to your ego, they have. I've eliminated each of them with my father's knife." He glanced down at the dead pilot. "Except for him. Now it's your turn."

Starling lowered his arms. "I'm an old man.

Chopra. Do what you have to do. But leave my daughter alone. She had nothing to do with any of this."

Carl Baxter cleared his throat. "Chopper? Hate to get in the middle of this, but there's the matter of the money. You go hacking Starling up into fish bait, how am I supposed to get what's left of his stash? We need him alive for a while yet. And my wife, too. She'll be his incentive to cooperate."

"Why did you marry my daughter, William?" Reed asked. "She was only twelve when you saw her in Chicago."

"I never even knew you had a daughter when I lived in Chicago," Carl said. "I first learned about her in the paper after you blew town, then later when your wife died. When I realized she must have turned eighteen, I tracked her down.

"And by the way, I'm not William Smith anymore. I don't work for a street gang, I don't associate with crooked cops. I have bigger fish to fry nowadays."

"You used Ella to get close to me."

"Fat lot of good it did. She hated you. Refused to talk about you. Blamed you for her mother killing herself, blamed you for everything and with good cause. We got divorced before two months went by, but I kept her in my sights and when I heard you were looking for her and your son, I got closer to her and you know what? She still hates you. When your first contact got to her house, she wouldn't even let him in the door, refused to listen to him, told him to tell you as far as she was concerned you were already dead. Good thing I came in the back way and…convinced her to be more agreeable."

Starling looked at Ella and said, "I wanted to explain all this so you'd understand. Nothing is really what it seems."

"You wanted to explain why you left me with a woman who beat me? Or did you want to explain how you were the cop who had the least to lose? Which?"

"You remember your mother's abuse?"

"It's about the only memory I have of her."

"She was sick—"

"And you left both of us. She was a bitter, unhappy drunk and you left."

"The others promised to take care of her, look after you, but they didn't. That's why they owed me. I kept my part of the bargain, I took the money and disappeared and let them all go on with their lives and act like heroes."

"And left your wife and children to carry the burden of your disgrace."

"She wouldn't take a dime of the money, wouldn't let me provide for you or your brother, wouldn't join me…all she wanted was to wallow in her misery."

"And who do you think wallowed with her?" Ella said. "At least I now understand why every dream I have of you ends up with you disappearing into a puff of smoke."

"I'm sorry," Reed said, and sounded genuinely contrite.

Ella said, "It doesn't matter. I have a feeling I gave up on you years and years ago." She turned her attention to Carl and added, "And *you* killed the first contact? *You* dumped that man in the vacant lot? I didn't have anything to do with it?"

"I didn't kill him. I just tied him up and left him at your place." He smiled to himself as he added, "Chopper found him before he could get free. They had a little chat and then Chopper carved him into pieces."

"You made me go with you. Why did you crash the car?"

"That wasn't my fault. You grabbed the wheel from me. You sent us off the road."

"No more talking!" Chopra spit, his voice deadly earnest. "The money isn't important. The past doesn't matter. Even if what you say is true, Starling, the men I killed were guilty and so are you." He looked at Baxter and added, "It's blood money. I will have this man's life in retribution for my father and—"

"Yeah, yeah, yeah," Carl interrupted. "Nice sentiment, good devotion, et cetera…but the fact is we have an agreement. You can do whatever you want with Starling as soon as he buys his daughter's life with what he's got left of the money. It better be a lot, too. She's been a ton of trouble. And let's not forget, he's the only one who can fly us out of here now that the pilot is dead."

For some time, as he'd tried to absorb everything that was going on around him and figure out a way to use the dynamics to his advantage, Simon had been aware of a noise coming from the forest to the west. Now it seemed they all became aware of it, because voices died down as everyone turned to look toward the bank of dense trees.

Chopper said, "What the hell?"

What the hell was right. Through a break in the trees something large and bright yellow came rumbling out.

"It's a school bus," Ella said.

Carl snarled. "Great, just what we need. Chopper, hold the knife lower before some busybody teacher with a cell phone sees it and calls the cops. Wait, prop the pilot up against the wheel, everyone look friendly or Eleanor isn't going to live long enough to have her baby."

Ella's gaze swerved from the bus to Carl so that the muzzle of Carl's gun now rested square on her forehead.

"You knew? You shot me with some drug, and you knew?"

"It's not my kid," Carl snarled.

"Well, thank goodness for that," she said.

"On the other hand, if *you* care about your baby's future, you'd better start playing the part of relaxed tourist." He waved the gun in a modest circle. "That goes for all of you. One false move and it's bye-bye, baby."

Ella, apparently taken aback by these words, looked down at her feet.

As they'd spoken, Chopra had pulled the dead pilot into a sitting position next to the helicopter wheel. Ella's father, who stood slightly tilted, due, no doubt, to his sprained ankle, watched the bus with a kind of fascinated horror. Simon knew how he felt.

"The damn thing is coming right toward us," Carl said. He lifted his free hand and waved at the bus, shouted for it to stop, but it kept coming, headed for the helicopter, sitting there with a full tank of gas.

The sun had moved around enough that the bus was now reflecting the light, but Simon began to get a funny feeling in the pit of his stomach.

"What's the matter with the damn driver?" Baxter sputtered. "He's going to run into the helicopter."

Hand held in front of him, Chopra took a few steps toward the bus. No doubt, with his size, he was used to imposing his will on anything and everyone, but even he was no match for a bus. When he saw it wasn't going to stop, he turned back to them. "We have to get out of the way!" he yelled as he grabbed Ella's father's arm.

"Let's get to that flat rock in the river. The damn bus can't roll over water," Carl said, yanking Ella along with him.

Simon realized that for a moment, he'd been pretty much forgotten. He dived for the abandoned revolver and rifle. By the time he was back on his feet, bullets pinged off the rocks around his feet. He quickly headed off in the other direction, running a zigzag pattern. It would do none of them any good to get back in the same kind of standoff again. He needed to find cover and plan a rescue.

The bus had left the relatively smooth ground of the riverbank and started across the larger rocks, which slowed it down, made it rock and lurch. As Simon ran past he saw there was no driver, no passengers he could see, but the side door was open. He turned to look back, knowing a collision was imminent. That's when he saw a man holding on to the spare tire mounted on the back bumper.

As Simon stopped to gape, the man let go of the tire and fell to the rocks. The bus kept going, but the way ahead was even rougher. It hit a rut that spun out the front tires. It recovered, but the course veered. Now it was aimed toward the falls instead of the helicopter.

Simon made a split-second decision to use the bus as a cover to approach the rocks where the others had fled. He changed his direction and took off after the bus. From the corner of his eye, he saw the newcomer jump to his feet, look around and make a decision to join Simon. They exchanged a brief glance. With a start, Simon recognized the man's wild black hair and lively eyes.

"Jack?"

"Miss me?" Jack said, drawing close.

Simon handed over the rifle and managed a laugh.

Meanwhile, the bus's movements grew increasingly erratic. It was only a matter of time before it got stuck in a new rut or broke an axle. Simon planned ahead how to stay clear when the damn thing fell over.

A moment later, the yellow vehicle seemed to rear up on its back tires. Both men slowed down, careful to stay out of sight behind it. It crashed down and rolled forward, but something had changed. The mystery was explained when the rear tires came up against what had caused the trouble—a downed tree lying across the bank. Somehow, the engine had become disengaged, and without sufficient power, the bus floundered against the tree, then flipped over on its side with a tremendous crash.

Simon dived for cover. As the clattering went on and on, he got back to his feet. Jack was right behind him.

"I had the pedal depressed with a branch," Jack said. "It must have snapped."

"You passed us outside a town called Twilight," Simon said.

"I did? You must have been the only vehicle I passed in a hundred miles. That bus was no Harley. The guy at the lot got the better deal."

"Listen," Simon said. "I don't think they know about you. If I give myself up, you might have a chance to take them out."

Jack regarded him with narrowed eyes. "That'll probably get you killed," he said at last.

Simon shrugged. "Do you have a better plan?"

"No. There's an emergency exit in the back of the bus. I could climb in with the rifle."

"Are you a good enough shot to take each out with one bullet?" Simon asked. "You'd have to damn near be a sniper."

Jack almost smiled. When he spoke again, his accent, which seemed to come and go like the wind, was back. "*Sí*, amigo. I think I can handle it. You just get Ella and her father out of the line of fire."

Simon paused in his efforts to help Jack open the emergency door. "You know about her dad?"

"Yeah. I followed your friends to Potter's place. I was too late to save the old guy. His wife was grateful I came along. She told me what I needed to know."

The door finally slid open, the noise it made covered by the crashing still going on inside the bus interior.

Jack immediately hoisted himself up into the opening. With the bus on its side, he'd have to step over the windows to get to the front and he'd have to do it without getting cut by broken glass or seen by Carl or Chopra.

Simon handed him the revolver, too. He didn't need it. He hoped Jack was half as good as he seemed to think he was. Then he put his hands high in the air and walked out of the shelter of the bus, knowing it was just as likely Baxter would shoot him dead on the spot as allow him to join them.

Chapter Sixteen

Ella saw Simon first as all three men were staring at the bus wreck and she was staring behind it, searching for him. She saw him step out from behind the metal carcass, his hands up in the air. Her heart grew heavy in her chest. There was no hope now.

Carl saw Simon in the next instant. She knew when he raised his gun what he intended to do.

"If you shoot him, I will not cooperate in any way," she said. "Neither will my father. Kill Simon and you might as well kill both of us, too." And she meant it. The waterfall wasn't that far away, just a dozen leaps and she could throw herself into the maelstrom. Sure, she'd die, but Carl was going to kill her anyway, she knew that.

Carl's smile disappeared, a reward in its own right. She glanced quickly at her father to see how he'd taken her ultimatum. Hard to tell.

"Chopper, go take care of him," Carl said. "We'll follow."

As Ella furiously reiterated her threats, Chopra furrowed his brow. He glared at her dad and then, acting so fast it was little more than a blur, slammed the butt end of his rifle into her father's chest. Without another word, he left.

Ella's father doubled over, cradling his arm, which he'd apparently used to ward off the blow. As she reached out to help him, Carl grabbed a handful of her short hair and pulled her head back, forcing her to look up into his face.

"You've been nothing but a giant pain since the day I met you," he said. His eyes bored into her like drills. The skin on her exposed throat burned as he ran the muzzle of the gun down her windpipe. "How dare you think you can threaten me into doing what you want?" He cocked the gun, the click like thunder next to Ella's ear.

And then all of a sudden, he threw her down to the rock. She looked up in time to witness her father jump to the next rock and then the next, almost falling as his bad ankle took the landing, his injured arm supported by his uninjured one. Each faltering leap took him farther out into the river, toward the falls. Carl lifted the gun, seemed to think twice about shooting a man he planned to get rich off, especially as he might fall into the river and be lost. Instead of shooting, he took a leap and followed.

And for some reason Ella would never understand, she followed, too.

SIMON WASN'T THRILLED about Chopra's steady, deadly advance. Behind the man, he witnessed Ella's father making a break for it, leaving Ella stranded with Carl, who had her head bent over backward. A surge of anger flooded his central nervous system—Tyler Starling truly was despicable.

But then Carl threw Ella to the rock and took off after Starling and then Ella popped to her feet and followed Carl.

Chopper and his knife were getting damn close. Seeing as Chopper really didn't know if Simon had a gun tucked away, he was taking a big chance. Probably figured it would take more than a puny revolver to stop him.

Come on, Jack, Simon muttered to himself. *Any time now.* The fact was that Baxter was out of reach of the rifle. That meant Jack could stop Chopra but not Baxter. That meant he had to do it fast so Simon could stop Baxter.

The big man covered ground very fast. There was no way around him to help Ella; Simon had to go through him. He called out, "Sanjay? What do you suppose your father would think about his own son avenging his life by killing innocent people? You said he was a man of honor."

"The girl is a Starling," Chopra said calmly. "She is tied to her father's evil."

"You've killed three men," Simon said.

Chopra held up the knife. "I'll soon make it four and then five and then it will be over."

"Don't you see how Baxter's corruption is corrupting you? You wouldn't kill me yesterday, but today, here you are, lusting for my blood."

"Not lusting," Chopra said, close enough now to come to a stop. "Just taking care of business."

Simon lowered his head and charged Chopra. He hit him in the chest and almost bounced off. The sun glinted off the kukri's blade as Chopra shifted it into his right hand. Simon stumbled backward, tripping over a boulder, sprawling on the riverbank, faceup. Chopra was there in a flash. The curved blade of the knife started a downward plunge.

Simon took an instinctive breath to prepare himself for the worst. Instead, the knife fell from Chopra's grip as his hand flew backward. Jack had hit the guy's palm. Chopra advanced, another shot and his leg crumbled. He stumbled, giving Simon the opportunity to hit him hard and heavy. Wounded, the big man fell to the rocks. Simon scampered to his feet, heart pounding.

Jack showed up. Chopra lay writhing on the ground.

Without waiting to thank Jack, Simon took off toward the waterfall.

CARL WAS AT LEAST twenty-five years younger than her dad and uninjured. It wouldn't be long before he caught up with him. Ella doubled her efforts, practically flying between leaps. Looking ahead, she saw her father had almost gained the last negotiable rock. She made the first of her last two jumps and looked up in time to see Carl grab her father's coat by the back of the collar. The waterfall was so close the noise was deafening and river water washed over the rocks, making them slippery. She fell to her knees as she landed.

Carl shouted something, but there was no way to hear what he said. He pointed the gun at Ella, his meaning clear. All they'd accomplished was moving the hostage situation out onto the river.

She turned in time to see Simon upriver, jumping between rocks, and despite the knowledge his appearance out here was likely to get them all killed, felt a surge of love for him. He was such a controlled guy, such a cop, and look at him, behaving like a man willing to die for a woman.

It took her a second to realize there was another man behind him.

She looked back at her father, who had inched closer to the edge of the rock, and she knew, she knew, he was about to make a sacrifice to protect her. If he was gone, she would be safe; only it wouldn't work that way.

Meanwhile, Carl looked as though he was trying to decide who to shoot first. His arrogance changed her blood into lava. It pulsed through her veins, surged through her heart, burned in her throat. With a guttural scream, she rushed him, shoving him with her shoulder, emulating a linebacker.

Carl's eyes registered stunned surprise at her audacity. He stumbled backward, seemed to catch himself, then slipped again as his feet came down on a patch of moss. A triumphant smile disappeared as he lost his balance. As he went over the edge into the water, his flailing hand caught hold of her father's jacket. The older man went down on his belly and slid to the brim. Carl released the gun and grabbed the rock.

Ella immediately clutched her father's arm. She pounded on Carl's fingers with her fists. He lost his grip on the rock, but the death grip on the jacket remained.

Her father's lips moved as he stared into her eyes. She couldn't hear over the blood rushing in her head and the river and falls—it looked as though he said *pocket*. She stuck her hand in her pocket and felt the rounded dome of the snow globe. For a second, the river became the ocean; she was dizzy and disorientated.

Her father shook his head furiously. She took a deep breath as his lips moved once again and she finally understood he meant his own pocket. Of course. His jacket had deep pouches on the sides with fold-over flaps. She'd seen him stuff a half-dozen things in those pockets over the course of the past twenty hours. Reaching in, she gouged herself on a fishhook before claiming the prize: his pocketknife.

She flipped the blade from the cover and began sawing on the cloth. Carl had managed to swing his other arm into position and now gripped the coat with both hands. Raging water pummeled his face, blurred his features. He sputtered and gasped. She tried not to look at him.

The cloth was too strong, and wet, maybe even stronger. She made holes and slashes, but it wouldn't tear. Her father slipped farther forward and she held on to him with one arm.

Then it occurred to her to use the knife to stab Carl's hands. She raised it and steeled herself, but before she could plunge the knife into his flesh, the material finally started to give way. Her dad managed to twist his body and she saw that he'd somehow undone the buttons while she hacked at the cloth. The jacket slipped off his arms and immediately disappeared into the river. Carl was visible for just a second before the raging water sucked his body under and he was gone.

She and her father got to their feet. He was pale, wet; his arm hung uselessly at his side. His chest heaved with the effort of the past few moments.

She reached for him, half expecting him to dissolve into mist.

He clutched her extended hand.

AFTER WITNESSING THE DRAMA unfold as he jumped between the rocks, Simon landed on the rock a second later. Ella turned to face him, the smile on her face illuminating the air around her. She threw herself into his arms and he caught her. It was over, she was safe. He kissed her face a hundred times. It was a miracle.

He'd cupped her cheeks and was staring into her eyes when something caught her attention. Her eyes grew wide. He glanced over his shoulder and found Jack had arrived and was standing behind him.

Ella's hands flew to her face; tears sprang to her eyes. She moved away from Simon and toward Jack like a sleepwalker. Simon had witnessed the expression she wore—the unabashed love, the depth of joy in her eyes. It had been directed at him a time or two—

He turned away from their embrace. Taking Starling's good arm, he helped the older man back across the rocks, vaguely aware that Jack and Ella followed close behind.

By unspoken and mutual consent, they kept going, past Chopra, whom Simon saw had been deftly wrapped in his own duct tape, past the over-turned hulk of the bus, all the way to the helicopter and the pilot, whom Simon and Jack laid aside. Simon did everything mechanically. If he'd wondered before about the depth of his love for Ella, he needn't wonder again.

He loved her. Prickly, sweet, secretive, open, happy, sad…it didn't matter, he just plain loved her from the tips of her whacked-out brown hair to the depths of her guarded heart. He'd never stopped loving her and damn it, he had a horrible, horrible feeling he never would.

And that was a burden he was going to have to find a way to live with because Jack's identity was suddenly crystal clear. He had to be Ella's lover, the real reason she'd been distant before their breakup. Since finding out what had happened the night she was taken from her house, Simon had attributed her behavior to the mess with her ex-husband and her father; he'd not seriously considered the possibility of a wild-card lover.

Until now.

"Can you fly us out of here with a busted arm?" Simon asked Starling. All he wanted to do was get the hell off this riverbank. If Starling couldn't fly the chopper, then Simon intended on walking back the way they'd come. In fact, now that he thought about it, that was a better plan. He looked around for the backpack.

The old man shook his head. "'Fraid not. But my son can, can't you, Jack?"

Jack, his arm around Ella's shoulders, grinned.

"Your son?" Simon said.

"My brother," Ella added.

Simon looked from one of them to the next as it finally dawned on him she hadn't reacted to the news Jack was her supposedly dead brother, which meant she'd recognized him out on the rock. "You remember your family?" he said. Happiness for her and the fact that Jack wasn't her lover left him a little stunned. He abruptly sat down on a rock. "Your memory came back when you saw Jack."

She shook her head as she dug in her pocket and withdrew the snow globe.

"It started when I saw you racing out to save me—again—and then it just kept building until the moment I thought Carl was going to pull my father into the water. I touched the snow globe in my pocket and the day we bought it—you remember, it was raining that day and cold—came flooding back. Everything else followed. You, me, Jack, my father—everything."

"And your baby?"

"Our baby," she said with a dazzling smile.

He ran a hand over his face. "Thank heavens."

She caught his hand. "Of course it's your baby. Who else but you?"

"What's this about a baby?" Jack said.

Ella laughed. "Later, big brother."

Simon needed to get everything out in the open. He tugged on her hand, ran his fingers across hers, afraid to let go of her. "Can you forgive me?" he asked. Her features blurred and he blinked his eyes.

"Oh, Simon. Forgive you?"

"I've misled—"

"Shh," she said, leaning down to kiss him. "I've been running scared and hurt and angry for most of my life, my darling Simon."

"And that's my fault," Tyler Starling said. "I made a deal with a bunch of thieves mostly just to escape a bad marriage. I thought everything would be okay once I was gone. I thought Ella's mother would take the money I offered her and start over, but she got worse. And I couldn't come back, I couldn't help."

"And I was not only eight years older, I was already in the military," Jack added. "I was no help."

Ella shook her head. "It's too late now to change any of that." She turned back to Simon, meeting his gaze, lowering her voice. "You're the one good thing that's happened to me and I almost destroyed it. What do you want forgiveness for? For reading the clues at my house right? For coming after me even though we'd broken up and I'd been acting like an idiot? For risking your life, for saving mine, for giving up your career—what exactly do you want to be forgiven for? For loving me?"

He pulled her into his lap and buried his face against her sweet neck. He held her so tight she probably couldn't breathe, but he didn't care. She was his.

It didn't even matter that Jack and Starling were standing there, watching. Nothing mattered but Ella.

And the baby that bound them.

Epilogue

Seven months later

Ella's last memory of a holiday meal consisted of her mother passing out before the turkey was cooked. When she'd woken up and found it burned to a crisp, she'd slapped Ella so hard her cheek stung for hours.

But that memory was fifteen years old and it no longer held the power to hurt. There were two reasons for that, and both of them were within eyesight right that moment.

First and foremost, there was Simon, currently decanting a bottle of wine, tall and strong and so handsome in his red sweater it took her breath away. He was a detective on the police force now; being involved in helping solve multiple murders had actually brought him to the attention of his superiors and he'd been promoted.

Did she wish he wasn't a cop? Sometimes, but

that was the weak her talking and Ella had learned not to kowtow to that weak self, to let her have her moment of gut-wrenching fear and then push on.

The second and no less dear reason lay asleep in her arms. Emily Rose, named after Simon's mother and grandmother, five weeks and one day old. Simon called her his miracle baby and who could argue that? Emily Rose had lived through more adventures while in utero than most people did in a lifetime.

Oh, there were other reasons, too. Jack alive— talk about a miracle. They'd invited him to join them for the holiday, and he'd said he would but expect a surprise. As everything about her brother was a surprise, she'd just smiled.

As for her father? Well, he sent cryptic post-cards on occasion and was trying to convince her and Simon to bring Emily Rose to some undis-closed location to meet him. Maybe. She'd have to think about it.

They hadn't told anyone the truth about her father. They'd created an alternate story to explain Chopra and Carl. Considering Simon's bent toward the straight-arrow approach, she thought he'd been extremely generous to agree to let her father continue on his trek. There was no one to return the money to, no one left to prosecute. The only survivor from the old days who knew the truth about what had really happened all those years ago in Chicago was Cal Potter's widow, and she had no desire to see her husband's memory besmirched.

In the end, none of the men who murdered Sanjay Chopra's father and brother got away with it. The big man, along with Carl Baxter's help, had exacted retribution on every single one of them.

For now, the smell of roasting turkey filled the house, and Simon approached with a glass of wine. Later that night, they planned to put Emily Rose to bed and then retire to the big whirlpool bathtub he'd installed for her birthday, telling her it was only fitting a mermaid have a sanctuary.

They had a private holiday celebration to conduct.

"Trade?" he said.

She lifted the drowsy just-fed baby from her breast, kissed her downy forehead and handed her to her father. Simon passed her the wine goblet as he accepted the baby, and their fingers brushed. The brief contact set her hormones mad, screaming like crazy.

"The baby is sleepy and it's still a while before my brother and your family are due," she said softly, loving the way his eyes flooded with desire at the sound of her voice.

"You're on," he whispered, and cradling the baby with one arm, reached down to pull her to her feet.

* * * * *

Be sure to pick up Jack Starling's story,
on sale in summer 2010.

Rancher Ramsey Westmoreland's temporary cook is way too attractive for his liking. Little does he know Chloe Burton came to his ranch with another agenda entirely....

That man across the street had to be, without a doubt, the most handsome man she'd ever seen.

Chloe Burton's pulse beat rhythmically as he stopped to talk to another man in front of a feed store. He was tall, dark and every inch of sexy—from his Stetson to the well-worn leather boots on his feet. And from the way his jeans and Western shirt fit his broad muscular shoulders, it was quite obvious he had everything it took to separate the men from the boys. The combination was enough to corrupt any woman's mind and had her weakening even from a distance. Her body felt flushed. It was hot. Unsettled.

Over the past year the only male who had gotten her time and attention had been the e-mail. That was simply pathetic, especially since now she was practically drooling simply at the sight of a man. Even his stance—both hands in his jeans pockets, legs braced apart, was a pose she would carry to her dreams.

And he was smiling, evidently enjoying the conversation being exchanged. He had dimples, incredibly sexy dimples in not one but both cheeks.

"What are you staring at, Clo?"

Chloe nearly jumped. She'd forgotten she had a lunch date. She glanced over the table at her best friend from college, Lucia Conyers.

"Take a look at that man across the street in the blue shirt, Lucia. Will he not be perfect for Denver's first issue of *Simply Irresistible* or what?" Chloe asked with so much excitement she almost couldn't stand it.

She was the owner of *Simply Irresistible,* a magazine for today's up-and-coming woman. Their once a-year Irresistible Man cover, which highlighted a man the magazine felt deserved the honor, had increased sales enough for Chloe to open a Denver office.

When Lucia didn't say anything but kept staring, Chloe's smile widened. "Well?"

Lucia glanced across the booth at her. "Since you asked, I'll tell you what I see. One of the Westmorelands—Ramsey Westmoreland. And yes, he'd be perfect for the cover, but he won't do it."

Chloe raised a brow. "He'd get paid for his services, of course."

Lucia laughed and shook her head. "Getting paid won't be the issue, Clo—Ramsey is one of the wealthiest sheep ranchers in this part of

Colorado. But everyone knows what a private person he is. Trust me—he won't do it."

Chloe couldn't help but smile. The man was the epitome of what she was looking for in a magazine cover and she was determined that whatever it took, he would be it.

"Um, I don't like that look on your face, Chloe. I've seen it before and know exactly what it means."

She watched as Ramsey Westmoreland entered the store with a swagger that made her almost breathless. She *would* be seeing him again.

* * * * *

Look for Silhouette Desire's
HOT WESTMORELAND NIGHTS
by Brenda Jackson, available March 9
wherever books are sold.

Copyright © 2010 by Brenda Streater Jackson

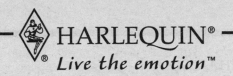

HARLEQUIN®
Live the emotion™

The series you love are now available in

LARGER PRINT!

The books are complete and unabridged—
printed in a larger type size to make it
easier on your eyes.

HARLEQUIN®
Romance

From the Heart, For the Heart

HARLEQUIN®
INTRIGUE

Breathtaking Romantic Suspense

HARLEQUIN®
Presents

Seduction and Passion Guaranteed!

HARLEQUIN®
Super Romance

Exciting, Emotional, Unexpected

Try LARGER PRINT today!
Visit: www.eHarlequin.com
Call: 1-800-873-8635

LPDIR09

HARLEQUIN® *Romance*®

The rush of falling in love

Cosmopolitan
international settings

Believable, feel-good stories
about today's women

The compelling thrill
of romantic excitement

It could happen to you!

EXPERIENCE
HARLEQUIN ROMANCE!

Available wherever Harlequin books are sold.

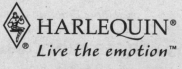

HARLEQUIN®
Live the emotion™

www.eHarlequin.com

HROMDIR09

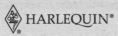
HARLEQUIN®

Invites *you* to experience lively, heartwarming all-American romances

Every month, we bring you four strong, sexy men, and four women who know what they want—and go all out to get it.

From small towns to big cities, experience a sense of adventure, romance and family spirit—the all-American way!

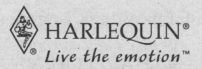

Love, Home & Happiness

HARLEQUIN®
Live the emotion™

www.eHarlequin.com   HARDIR09

HARLEQUIN®

Super Romance®

...there's more to the story!

Superromance.
A *big* satisfying read about unforgettable
characters. Each month we offer *six* very different
stories that range from family drama to adventure
and mystery, from highly emotional stories to
romantic comedies—and much more! Stories
about people you'll believe in and care about.
Stories too compelling to put down....

Our authors are among today's *best* romance
writers. You'll find familiar names and talented
newcomers. Many of them are award winners—
and you'll see why!

If you want the biggest and best
in romance fiction, you'll get it
from Superromance!

Exciting, Emotional, Unexpected...

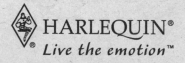

HARLEQUIN®
Live the emotion™

www.eHarlequin.com   HSDIR06

Harlequin® Historical
Historical Romantic Adventure!

*Imagine a time of chivalrous
knights and unconventional ladies,
roguish rakes and impetuous
heiresses, rugged cowboys
and spirited frontierswomen—
these rich and vivid tales will
capture your imagination!*

*Harlequin Historical . . .
they're too good to miss!*

HARLEQUIN®
Live the emotion™

Love, Home & Happiness

HARLEQUIN® *Blaze*™

Red-hot reads.

Harlequin® Historical
Historical Romantic Adventure!

HARLEQUIN® *Romance*®

From the Heart, For the Heart

HARLEQUIN®
INTRIGUE®

Breathtaking Romantic Suspense

Medical Romance™...
love is just a heartbeat away

HARLEQUIN®
Presents~
Seduction and Passion Guaranteed!

HARLEQUIN® *Super Romance*®

Exciting, Emotional, Unexpected

www.eHarlequin.com   HDIR09R2

Silhouette®

SPECIAL EDITION™

Emotional, compelling stories that capture the intensity of living, loving and creating a family in today's world.

Special Edition features bestselling authors such as Susan Mallery, Sherryl Woods, Christine Rimmer, Joan Elliott Pickart— and many more!

For a romantic, complex and emotional read, choose Silhouette Special Edition.

Silhouette®

Visit Silhouette Books at www.eHarlequin.com

SSEGEN06

Love Inspired SUSPENSE

RIVETING INSPIRATIONAL ROMANCE

Watch for our new series of
edge-of-your-seat suspense novels.
These contemporary tales
of intrigue and romance
feature Christian characters
facing challenges to their faith...
and their lives!

NOW AVAILABLE IN REGULAR
& LARGER-PRINT FORMATS

Steeple
Hill®

Visit:
www.SteepleHill.com

LISUSDIR10